BOOK 1

A Spark in the Dark

by Stacy Davidowitz
Illustrations by Victoria Ying

AMULET BOOKS
NEW YORK

Cataloging-in-Publication Data has been applied for and may be obtained from the Library of Congress.

ISBN 978-1-4197-2942-3

HASBRO and its logo HANAZUKI and all related characters are trademarks of Hasbro and used with permission. © 2018 Hasbro. All rights reserved.
Book design by Becky James

Printed and bound in China
10 9 8 7 6 5 4 3 2 1

Amulet Books are available at special discounts when purchased in quantity for premiums and promotions as well as fundraising or educational use. Special editions can also be created to specification. For details, contact specialsales@abramsbooks.com or the address below.

ABRAMS The Art of Books
195 Broadway, New York, NY 10007
abramsbooks.com

CONTENTS

CHAPTER ONE

OF CHAOS AND COMETS

lack, clack, clack! Hanazuki abruptly awoke to the clapping of moon rocks. She opened her eyes, and bouncing in a frenzy were her ten squishy friends, the Hemka. "Is there a snooze option around here?" she asked, exploding into a Moonflower yawn.

"Ya, ya, ya, yee-yoo," they replied.

"OK, great, clap me up in five."

Just as Hanazuki collapsed back into her sleeping bag, Red Hemka and Yellow Hemka pulled her out by her arms. Blue Hemka clung to her left leg. Pink Hemka clung to her right leg. Lavender Hemka screamed, "YEEEEEEE!" into her left ear. Teal Hemka screamed, "YOOOOOOO!" into her right ear. Orange Hemka, Green Hemka, and Purple Hemka stared at her like nervous spaceballs.

"And . . . I'm up! At the crack of moon! One of you please explain why you're all freaking out!"

Lime Green Hemka leaped into her lap, cowered in the crook of her armpit, and answered, "YA-YA-YEE-YEE-YOO-YOO-YAAAAA!"

"Aw, Lime Green, did you have a nightmare?"

He shook his head.

"A morningmare?"

Another no.

Hanazuki smiled and tickled him until he shouted, "Ya-ya-ya-ya-ya!" which sounded like laughter but was actually just the noise he made when he was having a panic attack.

"Well, whatever woke you all up—it wasn't a *real*mare. There's nothing to be afraid of. Look around!" Hanazuki swept her arm across the beautiful moon. To her left was the Rainbow Swirl Lake. To her right was a garden of Treasure

Trees. Up above were floating marshmallow clouds. "We are on the Light Side of the Moon, aka the *bright side* of the moon, remember? Here the rainbow waterfalls sparkle, and the Treasure Trees protect us, and there's no reason to be hiding in my armpit. Deep breaths!"

Lime Green stuck his head out from underneath Hanazuki's armpit and began to wheeze.

"That doesn't sound promising. Hold on." Hanazuki quickly gathered two giant Treasure Tree leaves and glued their edges together with goop. "Voila! It's a breathing bag! Breathe in and the leaves press together; breathe out and it blows up like a balloon. Helps steady your breath."

Hanazuki tried to pass the breathing bag to Lime Green, but Orange Hemka snatched it away.

"Very funny, Orange. Always a fan of your wackiness, but—"

Orange hopped away, the breathing bag clutched between his floppy ears.

"Oh, come on, Orange! It's way too early for running!"

Hanazuki leaped from her sleeping nook with Lime Green on her back and attempted to chase Orange down. They ran past a sleeping Talking Pyramid.

"Morning, Hana Z," he blurted, startled awake. "With the new day comes fresh problems, I see."

"Yup!" Hanazuki shouted behind her. "A small dose of morning chaos, though, usually makes for a chill-tastic afternoon."

"The storm before the calm."

"Ha, exactly!"

Orange slid down a crater, entering the moon's most lush and colorful Treasure Tree garden. Hanazuki followed. When she was finally at Orange's heels, he stopped short. Hanazuki crashed into him, and the breathing bag flew from his ears, catching on a red Treasure Tree branch totally out of reach. "Oh, moonshakes!"

she cried, then shook a fist at Orange. "Now see what you've done!"

Lime Green slid from Hanazuki's back and practically melted to the ground.

"Orange, why in the moon would you steal Lime Green's breathing bag?" she asked. "Don't you want to help? He's majorly freaked out. Over, um, *something*."

"Yoo-gee-yee!" Orange screeched, pointing his ears up to the bag.

"Yup, that's the bag."

"Yoo-gee-yee-cha," Orange screeched louder.

"Yup, it's stuck."

By now all the Hemka had arrived at the crime scene and were pointing their ears at the bag, too. What was this—early morning recess?! "Not. A. Toy," Hanazuki told them. "But hey, if you all want to play with the bag, then why don't you shapeshift into a ladder and grab it yourselves? You guys *do* shapeshift, right?"

All of a sudden, the red Treasure Tree let out a low, rumbling *"Mmmooooaaan."*

"Oh, no! What's wrong?" Hanazuki asked the tree, laying a gentle hand on its trembling trunk. The breathing bag was shaken free. It floated onto Lime Green's head. He did nothing but wear it as a hat.

"Buddy, use it," Hanazuki urged. "I *did not* just chase down Orange for nothing." But Lime Green didn't use the bag. He sat as still as a moon rock, his eyes halfway out of their sockets, looking at the branch where the breathing bag had just been. Same with the other Hemka. They couldn't keep their eyes from the shaking tree.

Just as Hanazuki began to follow their gaze, a treasure fruit smacked her on the forehead and knocked her flat on her back. "OW! What the—?" Red fruit of all sizes began dropping from the tree's branches onto her body. *Plop! Plop! Plop!* Before she could investigate the tree's health—Treasure Trees don't just shed their fruit!—she was buried under a fruit-salad avalanche.

6

Once the fruit stopped falling, Hanazuki shook her head and the treasure berries fell from her eyes. Through the barren branches she could see the sky, and in it were two fiery comets! They were about to collide! Dangerously close to her moon! *So* that's *why Lime Green was freaking out! That's why all the Hemka were freaking out!* "That's real. That's really real. And bad. Really, really real and bad."

Lime Green wriggled his way through the fruit to get back beneath her armpit. "Yo-yo-*yee-yee*," *he* whimpered.

Hanazuki's heart pounded with the fervor of a zillion exploding stars. A puddle of nerves, she couldn't move. "Do something," she uttered, trying to get herself to take action.

But Lime Green must have thought Hanazuki was insisting that *he* do something, since he obeyed by screaming "YAHHHHHH!" at the top of his little lungs.

Well, that worked, Hanazuki thought, climbing

out from beneath most of the fruit so she could cover her ears, if nothing else.

In a flash, Dazzlessence Jones was racing toward them. He was so shiny, it was blinding. Like a diamond skier, he dug the edges of his cowboy boots into the moon's surface to skid to a stop, clouding Hanazuki and Lime Green in moon soot. When the air cleared, he had his badge out. It read: MOON SHERIFF, CRIME HATER AKA CRATER, AND THE MOON'S MOST SHINY. "Hey *yo*! Did someone say, 'YAHHHHHH?'"

Hanazuki, in no mood for small talk, just pointed up.

Dazzlessence glanced at the sky and gasped. "*Goodness gracious, great balls of fire!* What're you doing comet-gazing, Hanazuki? There's no time for that! This is a disaster waiting to happen."

"I don't think the disaster's waiting," she said flatly.

"You're right. Let's stop those *great balls of fire* before they make *one great ball of fire* that destroys us all. You *in*?"

"Inner than in!" Hanazuki stood up with so much oomph that the rest of the fruit flew from her body. "What's the plan, Sheriff?"

"To the Safety Cave! *Wooo-eeeee!* This is *NOT A DRILL*!"

Hanazuki wanted to say, "That's the best you've got? Hide out in a cave?" But Dazzlessence had already flung her over his shoulder and was beelining it. The Hemka were frantically following. Swatting away low-riding marshmallow clouds and dodging fallen treasure fruit, they leaped through a Mouth Portal and exited next to the Safety Cave, where Sleepy Unicorn was fast asleep, inconveniently, in front of the door.

Hanazuki dropped from Dazzlessence's shoulder and tried to shake Sleepy Unicorn awake.

"Carrots with hummus," he mumbled, his eyes sealed shut.

"Sounds delish, but right now we need to get inside the Safety Cave!"

"Smoothie Crave."

"Nope." Hanazuki jumped on Sleepy's back, and then, as she spotted his magnificent horn, she was struck with a much better idea. "SLEEPY,

WAKE UP! ANYONE CAN HIDE, BUT YOU'RE THE ONLY ONE WHO CAN SAVE OUR MOON!"

"Oh, heeeey, Hanazuki," Sleepy Unicorn drawled, his eyes fluttering open. "What are you doing on my back? I don't give rides for free."

"I wasn't—UGH! I need you to look up. See those comets?"

"I see them very well. They're scary."

"That's why you're going to use your magic to stop them!"

"That sounds hard," he said, yawning. "Magic is hard."

"Well, so is MASS DESTRUCTION."

Sleepy blinked. "Fine, but you owe me one. And by 'one' I mean one moon cycle of uninterrupted REM sleep." He pointed his horn at the comets, made his concentration face, and fired his lightning magic. It spewed two feet in the air, probably at least fifty feet short of the comets, and then struck Lime Green on the way down. He puffed out like a cotton ball.

"Come on, Sleepy!" Hanazuki said. "You can do better than that."

"Zzzzzzzzz."

"NOOOOO! STOP FALLING ASLEEP!" Hanazuki waited five hopeful seconds, then sighed in defeat. "The Safety Cave it is." With help from the Hemka, she dragged a snoring Sleepy Unicorn away from the Safety Cave door. Just then, Little Dreamer appeared in a pink mouse onesie, his eyes shut and his smile content like always.

"Oh, hey there, snoozy man!" Hanazuki exclaimed. "You arrived just in time! Quick! Hide out with us!"

"Shee-shah nah zah-zah," he whispered, dropping a treasure in the shape of a comet.

It landed in her palm and instantly pulsed lime green. "Well, that's telling." The treasure would become a Treasure Tree when Hanazuki tossed it to the ground. But the color made her more worried. It expresssed her true mood and lime green meant fear.

"*Ain't nobody got time for treasure!*" Dazzlessence sang. In his dazzling diamond-boss glory, he shoved open the Safety Cave door and waved everyone inside. "*Let's go, let's go, let's gooooooo!*"

But it was too late. *BOOM! BANG! POP!* Hanazuki and her friends watched as the enormous comets collided within arm's reach of the moon. Debris rained from the sky. The marshmallow clouds roasted black. The rainbows turned upside down. The aftershocks triggered a moonquake. And the moon seemed to be hurtling through the galaxy, spinning and spinning and spinning on its axis.

Hanazuki grabbed Sleepy Unicorn's horn. The Hemka grabbed Hanazuki's ankles. And then, since Sleepy Unicorn was holding on to nothing, they were all flung in different directions.

"Whoaaaaaaaaaaaaa!" Hanazuki hurtled through the air, her fingers spread apart, desperate to catch hold of something, anything, to keep her secure. The next thing she knew, she was tangled in the twiggy branches of a Treasure Tree.

She caught sight of her friends. Little Dreamer was zipping toward a distant moon. Dazzlessence was tumbling toward the Rainbow Swirl Lake. Sleepy Unicorn was doing the Running Unicorn . . . in midair. The Hemka were being tossed around like microwave popcorn and screaming, "YA-YA-YA-YA!"

And then the spinning stopped. The moon was still. Gravity was back. Except Hanazuki's beautiful and safe Light Side of the Moon was now undeniably, devastatingly . . . dark!

CHAPTER TWO

DARK TIMES

Hanazuki squinted through a thick cloud of moon dust. "Lime Green? Dazzle? Sleepy? Everyone good?" Her heart racing, she climbed one moon- rubble mountain after another, until finally, at the peak of her eleventh hike, she heard the sublime symphony of "Ya-yoo-ya-yee!"s. Through the darkness, she could make out the outlines of her favorite squishy friends as they bounced toward her. Oh, so much relief!

"Hi, little guys! We survived!" she exclaimed, racing to meet them.

Lime Green leaped into her arms and then squeezed his eyes shut.

"Aw, don't tell me you're afraid of the dark," she nudged playfully.

Lime Green opened his eyes, then began to shriek.

"Whoa there! If the dark is so scary, then let's uh, uh . . ." Hanazuki looked for inspiration, her eyes hopping from whimpering Blue Hemka to brave-faced Purple Hemka to giddy Yellow Hemka. "Let's make it light!"

Lime Green stopped shrieking, apparently down with this plan.

"That's right, make it light," Hanazuki repeated, her mind whirling to figure out *how* to make it light—and fast, before Lime Green could let his vocal cords rip again. Make a bonfire! *Too dangerous.* Build a flashlight! *Too dark to find the materials.* Capture a star! *That's starnapping.*

All excited, Yellow Hemka ran around in circles. *Wait a sec*, Hanazuki thought. With his body the color of sunshine, he was the easiest of the Hemka to see! Maybe if there was more yellow around, their moon would shine a little brighter! "First step," she declared with confidence, "Find yellow goop."

Without so much as a question, the Hemka, minus Lime Green, bounced to the Goop Fountain to gather yellow goop. They came back with it surprisingly quickly, in buckets. Then they rocked side to side, waiting patiently for their next instruction.

"Great. Now, instead of using the goop to nourish the Treasure Trees, we're going to try something different. Step two: Smear the goop onto your skin so that you glow a little more, kind of like Yellow Hemka does!"

"Chee-chee ya-ya!" the Hemka replied, eating the yellow goop.

"No, I didn't say *eat* it. I said *smear* it."

The Hemka smeared the goop onto their lips, their tongues, and their teeth.

"Um, I think we're having a communication mishap."

The Hemka began to bounce up and down and sideways with glee. They weren't turning yellow. They weren't making the moon a little brighter. However, they *were* reveling in a yellow goop overdose. They danced and cheered.

Hanazuki's heart began to pound. Lime Green's eyes bulged in wonder and then . . . fear. As the Hemka began coming down from their yellow-goop frenzy, laughing in freaky unison—"Hee-ha! Hee-ha! Hee-ha!"—Lime Green lost it. He let his vocal cords rip louder than Hanazuki had ever heard before: "YAHHHHHHHHHHHH!"

Hanazuki rocked him gently. Teal shushed him. Orange shoved a piece of moon rubble into his mouth. He sucked on it like a pacifier for two glorious seconds before spitting it out and screaming again. It was ear-splitting.

"Hey, it's OK—I've got another idea," Hanazuki assured Lime Green. "While I figure out how to make it light, why don't you nap through the dark? I'll, uh, sing you a lullaby!" She cleared her throat. *"Hush little Hemka, don't throw a fit. When you wake, the moon will be lit."* As she sang, Lime Green began to relax in her arms. His breathing steadied, and then his body lightly twitched, which meant he'd finally drifted off to sleep.

"Hooray!" Hanazuki mouthed to the rest of the Hemka. Just as they went to sit down in a meditation circle to enjoy the peace and quiet, Dazzlessence arrived.

"Roger that," he yakked into a piece of roasted marshmallow cloud stuck to his shoulder, as if it were a walkie-talkie. "I've located them at Axis Rubble and Rock. Over 'n' out."

Hanazuki earmuffed Lime Green. "Hey, Dazz," she whispered. "Glad to see you. Well, I can *sort of* see you."

"SORT OF?!" He put his hands on his sharp hips and huffed. "'I can *sort of* see the diamond,' said NO ONE EVER. How am I supposed to sheriff the moon if y'all can't see me?"

Hanazuki backpedaled. "Ha! Jokes! I can totally see you."

"So, you dig my shine?"

"Dig it deep. Just like I dig your, um, 'walkie-talkie.'"

"His name is Marsh."

Hanazuki transferred Lime Green to Purple and faced Dazzlessence. She whispered, "Let's chat farther off where we can use our outdoor voices. I don't want to disturb—"

TOOOOOOT! Dazzlessence blew the whistle dangling from his neck.

Lime Green's eyes shot open and he began screaming. "YAHHHH! YAHHHH! YAHHHH!"

"Oh, come on, Dazz!" Hanazuki said. "Do you know how hard it was for me to get Lime Green down for a nap?"

"Nap? This is *no time for nap time!*"

With Lime Green still screaming, Hanazuki shoved her thumb into his mouth. He began to gnaw, which stung, but at least her eardrums felt less like they were melting. "Honestly, I don't know how much more darkness I can take," she confessed. "When do you think the light will be back? An hour or two?"

"Back? It's coming back?"

"Wait, it's NOT coming back?!" Hanazuki felt beads of sweat gather on her forehead. "The Light Side of the Moon is . . . going to be dark . . . FOREVER?"

"Forever-evah." Dazzlessence put his hand over Marsh and leaned in. "As far as I can tell, when the *comets colliiiiiided*, the explosion spun us 180 degrees off the axis. Looks like this is the way things are going to be around here from now on."

The Hemka stared at Hanazuki expectedly.

"Good thing light is so last season," she joked.

No one but Orange laughed.

Dazzlessence adjusted Marsh. It stuck to his fingers. "*Anyhoooooo*, we've been mandated to participate in a *mooooonwide cleanup of the comet debris.*"

"Mandated by . . . you?"

"*Huzzah-yeah!* Finally, some recognition!" He hugged her. "You know what? Let's keep it professional." He offered his hand for a shake, and in a miserable stupor, Hanazuki loosely shook it back. "Let's hop to it, y'all. *Comet debris ain't the waaaaay to be!*"

Dazzlessence danced the moonwalk away. Moments later, Hanazuki heard the *whoosh* of comet debris flying through the air and then the *kerplunk* of it crashing into a pile. She shuddered. The noise, the forever dark, Lime Green's screaming—it was too much. Each day brought new adventures, but this? *This?*

"Yooo-chee?" Lavender Hemka asked, apparently waiting for her to take the lead. In fact, all the Hemka were surrounding her, eagerly awaiting her orders.

Spiraling with worry and having nothing original to say, she clapped the Hemka to action. "OK, little guys! Let's hop to it. You heard the sheriff!"

Then, her mind in a haze, she began to walk away in the opposite direction of Dazzlessence.

"YEEE-ZEE-YA," the Hemka burst out in a panic.

"Oh, me?" Hanazuki said, stopping in her tracks. "I'm going on a solo mission to, uh, uh . . . to make stuff better."

"Yee-yoo? Cheeza?" Teal Hemka asked.

"*How* am I going to make stuff better?" she repeated, her mind clawing through the haze for an answer. "Well, if I can't bring you guys light, then . . ." She paused, watching them squirm in discomfort. "I'm gonna figure out how to make living in the dark not terrible."

The Hemka cocked their heads, clearly needing more assurance.

"And by 'not terrible' I mean AMAZING," she said. "After I'm done with my mission, living in the dark will be even better than it was in the light!"

The Hemka cheered, "YA! YA! YA!"

Hanazuki fist-pumped the air, a fake smile plastered on her face. "That's right! The dark isn't stark! It's cool! We're gonna live in it comfortably! Happily! Safely! Awesomely! This is the first best day of the rest of lives!"

The Hemka marched around her, chanting, "YA-YA-ZUKI! YA-YA-ZUKI!"

"I'm loving this *rah-rah Hemka-hood!*" she told them. "So, you guys clean up the comet debris, and I'll be back with answers! Let's rock!" Hanazuki skipped off aimlessly, and her face immediately fell. So did her pace—because her legs were shaking. She felt like a total fraud.

What was I thinking? she wondered. *I don't know anything about living comfortably in the dark. Is it even possible? What if it's not possible? What if we can never be happy again? Is this the first* miserable *day of the rest of our lives?!*

Hanazuki looked down at Lime Green, who was clinging to her calf like a koala. Apparently, her declaration hadn't had the same *rah-rah!* effect on him as it had on his fellow Hemka, and also, he didn't know what "solo mission" meant.

Before her pace could slow to an absolute stop, she heard the painful squawk of a comrade in need. "HANAZUKI! GET YOUR BUM OVER HERE."

Chicken Plant! Hanazuki felt a pinch of guilt. How could she not have checked on her favorite (well, only) plant friend who was also a chicken? She tossed Lime Green onto her shoulders, leaped through a Mouth Portal, and exited to another part of the moon, worrying all the while. What if Chicken Plant had been uprooted from the ground? What if she was a disheveled heap of feathers? What if she was detached from her stalk?!

Hanazuki arrived on the scene, but to her relief, Chicken Plant was still firmly fixed in the moon's surface. "Holy macaroni and chicken— you survived! Phew! I'm so proud of—"

"Yeah, yeah. Enough of the cute talk," Chicken

Plant cut in. "Right now, I want you to check out my night vision goggles."

"Oooh! Now *that's* what I call an idea! Night-vision goggles—wow! They are just what this moon needs to make living in the dark better! I've been slow-skipping around in search of ideas, and who would have guessed that here you'd be, delivering them!"

"Great story. Now, I'm going to need you to lean in real close."

"Of course!"

"Closer, *closer.*"

Hanazuki leaned in so close, her nose was touching Chicken Plant's stalk. She felt the stalk vibrate, which meant one thing, and one thing only.

"Oh, come on, CP! Are you *really* going to pounce at me for lunch?" But Chicken Plant's beak was already headed for her shoulder. "LIME! MOVE!" she shouted, throwing her hands up to protect him.

Lime Green flung himself off Hanazuki's

shoulders, landed on the ground, and then screamed in little traumatic bursts, "YAH! YAH! YAH!"

Hanazuki felt a weight lifted from her shoulders, literally, but also from her wrist.

"Ahem. Yuck. Not a Hemka." Chicken Plant spit with disgust, but nothing came out of her mouth. Instead, a bulge traveled down her neck. Her insides seemed to be doing the twist. She birthed an egg. It cracked open as soon as it hit the nest, and out tumbled Hanazuki's precious mood bracelet. It was gooey-gross with egg white.

"Really, Chicken Plant?"

"Sorry, not sorry."

Hanazuki drew in an deep breath and clasped her mood bracelet back onto her wrist. Then she began to make strides in the direction of *away.*

"If you do come across my night-vision goggles, though, just cluck-cluck at me," Chicken Plant called. "'Cuz I can't see so well."

"Welcome to the club."

Only a few strides later, Hanazuki felt her feet vibrate. A few strides more, and she felt her body pulsate. A few strides after that, she began to hear beatboxing. With every step, it was as though they were getting closer to a dance party. Her head began to bob. Her toes began to tap. Her hips began to swing. "Do you hear what I hear?" she asked Lime Green.

"Cha-ya," he said.

They followed the beats all the way to the foot of Talking Pyramid, who was decked out in supersize headphones, a wireless head mic, and a moon-gold chain.

"What up, moonstuds?" he asked. "This is your late-night rapper, Pyramid Scheme. I'm here to drop *knowledge like it's hot, knowledge like it's hot*." He broke into a beatbox that sounded like, "*Boots 'n' cats 'n' boots 'n'cats*." Then came the rap.

It's dark times, my brother,
Super dark times like this,
Make space that's bright,
In a place without light,
And you're feelin' total bliss.
Ev'rybody throw your hands in the air and
say, "YEAH!"*

Hanazuki threw her hands in the air and said, "YEAH!"

Lime Green stretched his ears in the air and said, "YA-YA!"

Talking Pyramid—*er*, Pyramid Scheme—took off his headphones. "Oh, hi there, Hana Z and Little the Lime! Didn't see you fanning out on the floor. Little Dreamer and I are so into my beats—I'm dropping them hotter than hot sauce—that we hardly notice a thing."

"Little Dreamer?" Hanazuki asked. "He's here, too?"

"Why, of course!" Pyramid Scheme pointed

up. "The absence of light makes the art grow stronger, right, Little the Dreamz?"

Little Dreamer, who had only ever flown by to deliver treasures to Hanazuki, was doing flips above Pyramid Scheme wearing his own set of headphones fastened to his large head. "Shee-shaw ooloo wiki-wiki," he whispered, his eyes closed and his smile contented like always.

"Huh. So, Mr. Scheme," Hanazuki began curiously. She wanted to know where he'd gotten headphones, a microphone, and also a moon-gold chain. But Pyramid Scheme had already fixed his headphones back over his ears and was rapping new lyrics.

Request "Call Your Moonfriend!" and
"Moonbeams in the Sky,"
   But only my original rhymes are gonna fly.
   My pop was the first Pyramid Schemer in
his day.
   He found his voice when the light went away.

The Great Depression had hit the moon,

A meteor struck, dented it like a spoon.

That's when my pop began to croon.

Y'all think it's too soon?

Nah. It's dark times, it's hard times, so let's bring in the bright.

Amirite? I'm right.

Hanazuki applauded, while Lime Green twitched his ears with enthusiasm. "Wow, I had no idea!" she told Pyramid Scheme. "Here I am in search of how to help my friends live comfortably in the dark, and here you are providing comfort!"

"There's no place for comfort in art," Pyramid Scheme replied.

"Oh."

"My art isn't supposed to relax you numb. It's supposed to affect you, make you think, make you feel, make you question your very existence."

"OH, THAT IT DOES," a sleepy voice drawled from around the corner. "PLEASE, HANAZUKI, HEEEEEELP!" It was followed by loud groaning.

"Excuse me, Mr. Scheme. I think I'm being summoned for a chat."

"See, that's why I do what I do. To spark discussion."

"Totes. We'll be back!" Hanazuki and Lime Green traced the groaning to Sleepy Unicorn, who was lying on the ground with his hooves over his ears. "Oh no, Sleepy! What's wrong?"

"Make him stop. Hanazuki, please, cream the Scheme."

"You don't like the music?" Hanazuki asked him, bewildered.

"Like?! I can't sleep. I'm tired. I can't sleep. Did I already say that I'm tired?"

"You did." Hanazuki stroked Sleepy's bedhead mane. "But, hey, you're the best power-napper I know. You can sleep through anything!"

"Not rap music," he said. "I was a competitive break-dancer back in ElemUnicorn School. The wordplay, the hot mics—it fires me up."

"Well, maybe this is the galaxy's way of telling you that it's time you bring back those moves!"

"I don't think the moon is ready for my dancing." He clapped his hooves together and then, in a sleepy daze, began to shake his bum. "My body's betraying me. No. More. Beats."

Hanazuki sighed. Now she had to crush Pyramid Scheme's dreams? His artistic vision? The art form of his heritage? Plus, so far, his music was the only thing on this moon that had distracted Lime Green from his fear of the dark. If it weren't for Sleepy Unicorn's suffering, she'd ask Pyramid Scheme to rap forever!

"You got this?" Sleepy asked.

"Me?" Hanazuki replied. "Oh, sure I got this. I got it all."

Sleepy stared at her, waiting for her to move.

Hanazuki stared back, waiting for a decision to

fall out of her mouth. Finally, in a panic, it did. "Look," she said, "if I'm going to help us all adjust to the dark, we're going to need to make some compromises. You and Pyramid Scheme can hash out the music problem yourselves."

"Ourselves?" Sleepy asked. "You're our Moonflower. This is your job."

"I'm pretty sure shutting down a block party isn't in my job description. Right now, you need to work out your differences with Scheme, and I need to finish my quest to help the *entire* moon. 'Divide and conquer' on three! *One, two, 'DIVIDE AND*—!'"

Lime Green threw himself across Hanazuki's feet. "Move, Lime Green." He began shrieking. Again. "Buddy, you have got to chill." The shrieking got louder. "This isn't healthy for either of us!" She put her pinkies in her ears. "Listen, Lime. Our moon is dark. I know that's scary, but this is an amazing opportunity for you to face your fears."

"YA-DA CHEE-CHAH," he shouted.

"Awesome. Now face them!" Hanazuki nudged him from her feet. He climbed to her neck. She peeled him from her neck. He jumped on her back. She swatted him off her back. He swung on her arm. She tickled him off her arm. He clung to her ankle. "ARG, I CAN'T TAKE IT ANYMORE!"

She plopped Lime Green onto Sleepy Unicorn's back. "Take Lime Green, Sleepy—talk it out, dance it out, whatever. You do that and I promise you won't be sleepless for long."

"How long?" Sleepy asked, his eyebrows twitching to the beat. "A second? A minute? An hour? A day? A week? A month? A year? A decade? A cent—"

"Exactly," Hanazuki said, committing to nothing.

Lime Green started to sob.

"Look, Lime, I'm . . . it's—" She wanted to tell him that she'd be back. That this short break was for the best. That it was OK to feel afraid. But all of her words seemed to get clogged in her throat, maybe because she wasn't convinced they were true. She used all of her strength to keep her head held high, and then for some reason, she broke into a cold sweat. "Never mind," was all she managed to croak.

Dejected and heartbroken, Hanazuki wandered off alone. *What is wrong with me?* she asked herself. *Sleepy's right—I'm a Moonflower and I've helped no one at all. What am I doing? Where am I going? What will my friends think when I fail them? How will they ever trust me again? How will I ever trust myself again?! Ahhhhhhhhhhhhh!*

"Shape up, Hanazuki!" a voice called from behind. "The moon can't have you freaking out, too!"

Hanazuki turned around and spotted Mirror Plant, its face the same as hers. "Me? Freaking out? Ha!" Hanazuki clasped her hands behind her head. "I was just giving myself a pep talk. Now that I'm home free, I'm cool as a cucumber in a cave."

"Cucumbers in caves? They ain't a thing."

"Oh yeah? Well, why don't we head to a cave, curl up in little crying balls, and see for ourselves?"

"Oh, Lordy. You're not going anywhere. You're paralyzed with fear."

"That's ridiculous! What makes you say that?"

"I literally mirror back your thoughts and feelings."

"Oh. Right. But still!" Hanazuki went to lift her foot, but her kneecaps were shaking too hard. "Look. I'm fine. I'm the fine one. Everyone else is freaking out. Lime Green's scared of the dark. Chicken Plant's starving. Sleepy Unicorn can't sleep. Talking Pyramid's on the brink of a noise violation. Dazzlessence thinks a roasted marshmallow is a walkie-talkie. But me?"

"Listen, Hanazuki. It's simple: You can't help your friends cope with the dark on your own."

"So why does everyone expect me to?"

"Because you expect yourself to." Mirror Plant mimicked her: "*I'll help. Don't worry. I'm on it. I got this.*" She slipped back into her normal voice. "Do you, Hanazuki? *Do* you got this?!"

"Ugh, not really, no."

"That's what I thought. You need H-E-L-P."

"But from who? Everyone on the Light Side is a hot mess! Unless . . ." Hanazuki stood tall, and felt as though moon rocks were being tossed from her shoulders. "I've got it! But *for real* this time! Are you thinking what I'm thinking?"

"Always," Mirror Plant said. "Bon voyage."

CHAPTER THREE

HELLO, DARK SIDE?

Hanazuki stood in front of a snoring Mouth Portal, its tongue lolling out like a red carpet. "Mouth Dude, I need to be transported to the Dark Side stat."

The Mouth Portal let out a spastic snore.

"Cool. And . . . to the Dark Side, here I come!" She stepped onto the edge of the limp tongue and tried to haul herself up. "It's like climbing up a moonslide, just a bit more slippery and—GAH!" She lost her grip and fell. "Maybe I just need some momentum." She backed up, jogged forward, and leaped toward the portal. She landed at the top of the tongue, then slid down it, getting a full body lick. "Third time's a charm, right?" She backed up *really far*, sprinted forward *really fast*, and dove inside. Just as she went to kick her legs inside, the Mouth Portal hocked up a hairball from Sleepy Unicorn's shedding mane, and Hanazuki was sent flying to the ground. "FINE, I'LL WALK!"

As Hanazuki trudged toward the Dark Side, the Mouth Portals began to drool, coating the ground. She kept her arms out like wings—every step a balancing act. The mouth slime levels were rising. Above the tops of her shoes. Up to her ankles. Up to her calves. She tried to push on, but only a quarter of the way there, the mouth slime was up to her knees. There was no way she could finish on foot.

Hanazuki hadn't expected journeying to the Dark Side of the Moon to be smooth sailing, but she hadn't expected it to be a phlegmy shipwreck either. Flooded with frustration, she sat inside a washed-up, hollow moon rock shaped like a donut and tried to think of an alternate travel plan. If only Maroshi, her chilled out Moonflower friend from a water-based moon, were here instead of surfing the galaxy. Surely, he'd know how to travel in rising mouth slime. He'd boogie board. He'd sail. He'd tube. *Tube! That's it!* Hanazuki pushed the hollow moon rock into the mouth slime, dove back inside, and began to move. Not *tubing a lazy river and wishing for a treasure-fruit smoothie* kind of moving. *Waterslide* kind of moving. "Fourth time's a charm, oooh, baby!" she cried into the atmosphere. "Thanks, Maroshi, for the inspiration! Sending you hugs through the galaxy!"

Watching the stars whir by, Hanazuki brainstormed questions for Doughy Bunington, an ex-Light Sider turned Dark Sider. *What was it like adapting to the Dark Side? Any tips for coping? What are the perks of the dark? Any advice for Lime Green? Can you TELL ME EVERTHING?!* She couldn't wait to hear his insight.

Hanazuki mouth-slime rafted along. She pummeled down craters. She ripped through

rubble. She conquered thrashing waves. Then, halfway round the moon, she washed ashore at the barrier where the Light Side of the Moon met the Dark. Soaked and excited, she pushed herself out of the tube. She felt entirely turned around. Seasickness? No. Something was . . . off. She gave it a second, and then, as her eyes began to burn, it hit. The Dark Side was unmistakably *light*.

On the rare occasion Hanazuki had crossed over to the Dark Side, it had been creepy, but seeing it lit was somehow even creepier. The bushes were jagged. The ground was cracked. The paths were overgrown with gray grass. Bleak Mouth Portals hung in the sky like scary masks. Everything needed a paint job.

"Just find Doughy, have a quick chat, then leave," she mumbled, convincing her trembling legs to move forward. "Find Doughy, have a quick—AAHHH!" Hanazuki tripped over a thick, reptilian tail. She face-planted, and then rolled over onto her back. Gazing down at her was a toddler T. rex–like Mazzadril with an eyepatch.

"*RAAAAAAAAAAWR.*"

Hanazuki's slime-drenched hair instantly dried. "Oh, heeeey, cute little Mazzadril with probably super scary Mazzadril parents," she cooed. "I was just leaving." She tiptoed backward, slowly, carefully, waiting for a chance to run for it. But then the toddler Mazzadril began to whimper.

She paused, pulled in two directions. Her brain was telling her to flee, but her heart was telling her to help. *Heart or brain? Brain or heart? AGG!* "What's wrong, little dude?" she asked, her mouth making the decision for her. The Mazzadril covered his face with his paws. "Are you—waaaait, no way—do you not like the light?!"

"*RAAAAWR. RITE RIS ROO RITE.*"

"The light is too bright? That's—wow! Do you know what the Light Siders would do for this light? On our side of the moon, we're totally stuck in the dark and we have no idea how to function. We're going through the same confusion as you, but flipped! How crazy is that?!"

"*RAWR*-AZY." The toddler Mazzadril began to daydream, his beady eyes like a movie screen, reflecting the good old days of the dark Dark Side of the Moon. Hanazuki watched him and his family frolic around the darkest parts of the darkest forests, plucking bushes and overturning moon rocks for bug snacks. They played catch with moonstones and clawed their initials into tree stumps. But then, as mealtime approached, what started as a family-friendly comedy quickly turned into a horror film of fang-bearing, limb-tearing, bone-licking madness. The toddler Mazzadril, though, he was different. He munched on moonweeds. Was he allergic to meat? Or was he maybe an herbivore?

The toddler Mazzadril blinked, and he was instantly snapped out of his daydream, tears streaming down his snout. "REE RISS RA RARK."

Hanazuki's heartstrings tugged her toward him, and before she could stop herself, she was patting his scaly side. "I know. I know you miss the dark. It can't be easy dealing with this. At least you're not alone, right? You have your family?"

"REE RALONE ROW."

"Why are you alone now? Did your family leave you?"

The toddler Mazzadril nodded, then opened his mouth. Where other Mazzadrils had fangs, he had stubby flat teeth. "REE RAVE RO RANGS!"

"Oh, Toddler Mazz. Can I call you that—'Toddler Mazz'?"

"RES."

"Sweet. So, Toddler Mazz, is that why you eat plants and not moon creatures? Because you have no fangs to chew the meat up?"

He nodded again. "REE REIRD. REE RON'T RELONG."

"You're not weird. You're special! I'm sure your family loves you and they're coming back for you. Just hang tight." Right on cue, a whole family of Mazzadrils—a mama, a papa, a grandpapa, two kiddos, and a baby—clawed through a set of bushes and clomped toward them. Hanazuki wanted to say, "See? There they are!" But instead, she froze. She'd just seen a Mazzadril's most precious hunting memories. She wasn't their pal. She was their *lunch*. "I taste gross," she blurted out, dropping to her knees. "Please don't eat me!"

But the Mazzadrils clomped past her to the shade. They weren't interested in hunting. They were interested in getting as far from the light as possible, even if that meant burying themselves in the moon earth. Which was exactly what they did.

"REE RATE RA RITE RITE! REE RATE RIT, *RAAAAAWR!*" Presumed translation: "WE HATE THE BRIGHT LIGHT! WE HATE IT, *RAAAAAWR!*"

Arms outstretched, Toddler Mazz tottered toward his papa. But because his papa's head was buried in the moon earth, he accidentally kicked his son in the stomach, sending him flying into Hanazuki's lap. There was no coming back from that blow. Toddler Mazz rested his head on Hanazuki's shoulder and began to sob. Droplets the size of treasure fruit soaked her from her toes to her hair. "Oh, little buddy, it's OK!" She cradled him. Hugged him. Petted his back. Just like she would with Lime Green.

All of a sudden, Hanazuki felt a wave of guilt ripple down to her belly button. How could she be comforting Toddler Mazz after having left Lime Green behind? Did Lime Green feel abandoned by Hanazuki just like Toddler Mazz felt abandoned by his family? Did Lime Green also feel like he didn't belong? She had to find Doughy and then get back to Lime Green stat! But there was no way she could leave this cuddly, weepy guy behind.

"That's it," she told Toddler Mazz. "You're coming with me. If you feel like you don't belong here, and I feel like I don't belong here either, then we'll not belong together, and instead, we'll belong to each other."

Toddler Mazz stifled his sobs. Then he wiped the dripping snot from his snout and clapped his claws together. "REE RUV RU," he said.

Hanazuki's heart grew a size. "I love you, too," she said back. Finally, she was being helpful! Finally, she was putting her Moonflower skills to use! The whole helping thing felt better than wiggling her toes in the Rainbow Swirl Lake. Which, let's be clear, felt amazing. "Hop on my back!" she said. "Next stop: Doughy Bunington! Have you met him? He's wonderful. He's a hotdog in a bun who wears a crown."

Toddler Mazz broke into a fangless grin.

"It goes without saying that you can't eat him, not even his meatless bun, but I bet if you *RAWR* really nicely, he'll give you a scone from his pastry farm."

"RUPCAKE, REEZ."

"Sure. For you, a cupcake."

Hanazuki made strides toward Doughy Bunington's pastry farm, with Toddler Mazz on her back. A couple of miles later, she was desperate for a breather. She led Toddler Mazz inside a cave to drink water, reapply sunscreen, and go to the bathroom. But just beyond the dark entranceway, the cave was brightly lit. The top had been blown off, probably from the comet collision, and short-circuiting in the spotlight was Basal Ganglia, a maniac brain with eyeballs.

"Hey, Basal Ganglia," Hanazuki said. "Want me to move you into the shade?"

"Throw me in the shade? NEVER!" A spark flew from his frontal lobe. "Eat. Sleep. Breathe. Suntan." Sparks flew from his cerebrum. "DON'T FIGHT THE LIGHT."

"Remember me? I'm Hanazuki."

"Bow to me, Kazanaki."

"It's *Hanazuki*."

"Kiss my feet, Nazakuni."

"You don't have feet."

He looked up through the open sunroof. "Repeat after me: 'Blessed be ME, the FUTURE RULER of THIS MOON and EVERY MOON and all the MOON CREATURES and

MOONFLOWERS and MOOD PLUMES and MOONCAKES. AMEN!'"

"Blessed be ME, the future ruler—"

"I said, 'ME.'"

"So did I."

"LONG LIVE BASAL GANGLIA!" His entire body, which was just a brain, suddenly went up in flames. "MWAH HA HA HA HA!"

"BASAL, *NOOOO*!" Hanazuki waved her arms at him, but she was doing the opposite of helping. She was fanning the flames. "Toddler Mazz? Anything?"

Toddler Mazz took a big breath, then shot smoke through his nostrils. The fire was instantly extinguished. A crispy Basal Ganglia emerged from the cloud of smoke, and he was somehow still laughing. "MWAH HA HA ha hee hee hooo hooooo—" The laugh dissolved into a wheezing cough.

"Alright, buddy brain, you're coming with us," Hanazuki said. "Next time you spontaneously burst into flames, trust me, you're going to want friends by your side."

"Sure, yes, *friends*," Basal Ganglia said, raising a singed eyebrow. "Friends I will RULE OVER and make ALL THE RULES for."

"Yup, that's the definition of a ruler."

"A twelve-inch RULER with a lot of centimeters."

"Yup, that's the *other* definition of a ruler."

"Tape measures MUST surrender."

"Oh boy." Hanazuki tossed Basal Ganglia and Toddler Mazz onto a makeshift moon-rock sleigh and dragged them for miles and miles, or as Basal measured them, "RULERS and RULERS," until finally they reached the pastry farm. Doughy Bunington was there in sunglasses, dripping with sweat and flapping his bun over a section of blueberry cupcakes.

"DOUGHY!" Hanazuki raced toward her friend.

Startled, Doughy accidentally knocked into a cupcake that knocked into another cupcake that knocked into another cupcake, until an entire row fell over like dominos. "Oh, Hanazuki, what a disaster!" He cried. "I'm trying to fan my cupcakes, but the light is too strong. The icing keeps melting. I had messages on them: 'Happy Birthday' and 'Happy Bat Mitzvah' and 'Happy Sweet Sixteen' and 'Happy Cake Cleanse.' Now look at them. They're smudged and ugly and sad, sad, sad!"

Hanazuki looked at the drooping cupcakes, trying to think of something positive to say. "Well, I bet they still taste good." She plucked a particularly tasty-looking one and brought it to her lips.

Doughy knocked the cupcake from her hand. "Taste good? HA!" He pointed at it on the ground. "Do you see the cream cheese icing? It's *curdling*!"

"*Is it*?"

"Of course it is!" Doughy took his sunglasses off to examine it, but then began to examine his body instead. He cringed. "I've grown so used to my muted colors. Now look at me. My mustard lips are bright yellow! My auburn body is bright red! My amber bun is bright beige! I don't even know who I am anymore. *Who am I*?!"

"You're Doughy. You're yourself, but amplified!"

"Amplified? I'm too shy to be amplified." Doughy slipped his sunglasses back on. "I think I'm experiencing a mid-light crisis."

Hanazuki sighed. "Well, if it helps, I know how you feel, sort of. Just like the Dark Side of the Moon is light, the Light Side of the Moon is dark."

Doughy's eyes turned into sparklers. "It's dark? *How* dark?"

"Like *dark* dark."

"OH, FUNFETTI, LET'S JUMP FOR JOY!" He grabbed Hanazuki's hands and jumped up and down. "What FANTASTIC news! You came all this way for US!"

Hanazuki winced. "Actually, I came to you for answers—"

"YES!"

"Yes, what?"

"YES. The answer is, Y-E-S spells YES!" He waved Toddler Mazz and Basal Ganglia over and didn't even blink at their icing mustaches. "Of *course* we, the Dark Side moon creatures, will inhabit your side of the moon."

"Uhhhhhh . . ."

"I know just the spot for my new and improved pastry farm! YIPEE!" He proceeded to launch into a laundry list of housing needs and dietary needs and climate needs and a lot of other needs.

Meanwhile, before Hanazuki could protest or ask any one of her urgent questions or remind Doughy that he was *still exiled*, Toddler Mazz's entire family clomped back to the scene. Hanazuki was lifted into the air by the *RAWR*-ing Mazzadrils, who still had no interest in eating her—thank the moon gods—but were apparently also super stoked about Doughy's unsolicited plan.

"Three Roars for Hanazuki!" Doughy cried.

"*RAWR! RAWR! RAWR!*"

Hanazuki felt anxiety rolling in her stomach. "UH, GUYS? Let's PAUSE for a sec. I need *YOUR* advice. I need *YOU* to help *ME.* NOT THE OTHER WAY AROUND!"

But no one seemed to hear.

"On your mark, get set . . . TO THE DARK!" Doughy bellowed.

And in a snap, they were off.

CHAPTER FOUR

ONE BIG CHAOTIC FAMILY

WAIT UP," Hanazuki called out as the Mazzadrils leaped over a crater. Doughy Bunington was riding Papa Mazzadril's back, Basal Ganglia was riding Grandpapa Mazzadril's back, and Toddler Mazz was riding a kiddo Mazzadril's back, and since Hanazuki wasn't riding anyone's back, she was left in the scorching light all alone. "YOU CAN'T GET THERE BEFORE ME! SERIOUSLY!" she continued to call. "I NEED TO WARN MY FRIENDS YOU'RE COMING! LIME GREEN'S ALREADY FREAKING OUT! DO YOU WANT HIM TO FREAK OUT EVEN MORE?"

Nothing. The Dark Siders were already too far

ahead, too excited, too ready to inhabit the Light Side of the Moon. To catch up with them, Hanazuki would need to take a shortcut. She wandered around in search of a Mouth Portal with a dry mouth, and she luckily found one on the other end of Doughy's farm. She leaped inside and was transported to her home side of the moon.

"I'm baaaack, Lime!" She landed ankle-deep in mouth slime in another one of her lush Treasure Tree gardens. Well, it wasn't so lush anymore. There were comet shards sticking out from the tree trunks. Branches were frail. Leaves were crunchy. And to make matters worse, Doughy was somehow sloshing around, picking the last of the treasure fruit.

"Don't do that!" Hanazuki cried.

"Do what?" Doughy asked, plucking the last fruit from a wilting blue Treasure Tree.

"THAT," Hanazuki said. She snatched the blue treasure fruit from his basket and tried to reattach it to the tree. Unsurprisingly, it didn't work. "Also, wow, you got here quick. Where's the rest of the gang?"

"Oh, you know. We're all doin' our own thang." He plucked the last fruit from a wilting yellow Treasure Tree.

Hanazuki's stress levels nearly went bananas. "Hey. You. Doughy. I didn't bring you over here so you could do your 'own thang.'"

"Oh. Well, then, why did you bring me over?"

"Uh, technically I didn't." Doughy blinked. Embarrassed, Hanazuki plowed on. "Look, now that you're here, do you think you can be of some help?"

"I love getting help."

"Not what I said."

"What's the pay rate?"

"There is no pay rate. AGGG! How do I put this? Oh! Since all you Dark Siders are plagued with the light, and us Light Siders are plagued with the dark, we all have something to bond over."

She took an anxious breath. "Please tell me that makes sense."

Doughy tapped his chin in thought, but Hanazuki didn't give him the chance to respond. She leaped in the air and landed with a splash, buzzing with a revelation. "You know what? I'll spin it as a mentor program! I'll buddy the Dark and Light Siders up. You with Sleepy, Toddler Mazz with Dazz, Basal with Chicken Plant . . . Who's to say we can't live in harmony! Who's to say we can't thrive as One Big Happy Family!" She laughed. "I don't know why I didn't think this way before. It's so obvious! Of course we should be joining forces. TOGETHER we are going to DOMINATE THE DARK!"

"OK, I'll grow Sleepy a muffin."

Hanazuki smacked her forehead. "No. No muffins." She pointed at Doughy's fruit basket. "Right now, we need to be *nurturing* the trees. Not taking what's left of them."

"Well, I'm sorry," Doughy said, hugging the basket to his hotdog middle, "but how else am I supposed to grow *blue*berry cupcakes and *red* apple turnovers and key *lime* pies on my farm in front of Chicken Plant."

"WHAT?! NO!" Hanazuki exclaimed. "You can't go *anywhere near* Chicken Plant. She's the one who exiled you, remember? For eating her wings?"

"There's nothing to be worked up about. Her wings are all grown back."

"And you know that HOW?!"

"I saw her. It didn't go so hot. She tried to eat my bun. Also, she said you're toast. Which is confusing. You're not cloaked in bread at all. Does Sleepy like lemon zest?"

"Stay here. Don't move. And no more picking fruit!" Hanazuki was so nervous. She desperately wanted to find Lime Green, but first she sprinted over to Chicken Plant to make sure she was OK, and also to explain to her that Doughy Bunington had never been granted permission to return to the Light Side or to grow a new pastry farm right in front of her face. Moments later, she arrived to find Toddler Mazz sitting within pouncing range of Chicken Plant, smiling like a clown. "Well, this is a recipe for disaster," she said, her heartbeat kicking up a notch.

"It's fine," Chicken Plant squawked coolly, then *immediately pounced at Toddler Mazz.* He disappeared inside her beak. His eyepatch and flat teeth pressed against the inside of her neck. He thrashed and clawed about as he traveled down into her body, while she screeched in so much pain that her feathers leaped from her skin.

"I can't look, I can't look," Hanazuki muttered, shielding her eyes.

"Well, how convenient that you get to look the other way while this bugger uses my insides like a playground," Chicken Plant squawked. "I will not CLUCK for this!"

"Well, here's an idea for next time: DON'T EAT HIM."

"So, this is *my* fault?" Chicken Plant asked. "I'm hungry, Hanazuki! My pouncing game is not on point in the dark, so I have to take what snacks I can get!"

"He's my friend. So, not a snack."

"Is *Doughy Bunington* your friend now, too? If a filthy animal ate a part of you, how would you feel learning that he was about to be your newest neighbor?! Hold it. Ow. Ow. OWWWWWWW!" An egg dropped into the nest and Toddler Mazz burst out of it, a huge smile on his face. He crawled to the same place he'd been when Hanazuki arrived, directly in front of Chicken Plant's beak. "Scat!" she squawked at him. "My organs are not a jigsaw puzzle, you one-eyed, indigestible Mazz!"

"RESS RAY RAWR," he roared happily.

Then Chicken Plant ate Toddler Mazz again.

"AGG! Come on, really?!" Hanazuki said, storming off. "We're done here."

"Get Doughy outta here, Hanazuki," Chicken Plant squawked after her. "I'm warning you. He puts his farm in my face and I will inhale every last one of his dumb, delicious pastries! Ow, ow, OWWWWWW!"

Hanazuki tuned her out, distracted by an unsettling parade of Hemka carrying Basal Ganglia on a flat moon rock. Where is *Lime Green?* she wondered as she spotted Yellow Hemka, Green Hemka, Orange Hemka, and Lavender Hemka. Lime was nowhere in sight. "FASTER, MWA-HA!" Basal barked at them. "GOOD. THIS IS FAST. NOW FEED ME BRAINTEASERS!"

"Yee yoo chatza?" Lavender asked.

"To get to the other side! NEXT!"

"Ya-yoodoo-tzee?" Orange asked.

"Two goats and a school bus! NEXT."

"Uh, guys?" Hanazuki said, jogging up to them. "You don't have to do whatever Basal Ganglia says. You know that, right?" Ignoring Hanazuki, the Hemka marched into a crater sandbox, lowered Basal to the sand, and began to build him a sandcastle. "All I'm saying is that he's a selfish, wacked-out brain. Please take everything he says with a grain of salt! Or, like, a lot of grains."

"I GAVE THEM MOON SHRUBS FOR THEIR EARS SO THAT THEY CAN'T HEAR YOU," Basal shouted at her. "NOW WHO'S THE FOOL?"

"I dunno, that's a tough one."

Suddenly, a glowing, blue message ball floated down from the sky. Hanazuki held it between her hands, staring at it with a mix of curiosity and dread. So far, she'd only ever exchanged interlunar messages with Kiyoshi, her fellow Moonflower, who was always anxious and generally needed Hanazuki to solve his moon's problems.

Hanazuki began to gnaw at her fingernails. Right now, her moon needed her. She could only help so many of her friends at once. But what if Kiyoshi needed her more? *Do the right thing,* she told herself, aiming to throw the space spam against a flat moon rock. *Crack open the message.*

Then, at least you'll know what you're dealing with.

Just as Hanazuki went to unleash the news, another bunch of Hemka rushed past her, shoving her against a pile of moon rubble. The message slipped from her fingers and floated up into the atmosphere.

"No! Wait!" Hanazuki cried. "Come back, space spam!" Her chest tightened. Even if she didn't have the time to put out interlunar fires, she at least wanted to know what Kiyoshi's fire was! She stared after Purple Hemka, Blue Hemka, Pink Hemka, and Teal Hemka. The two kiddo Mazzadrils clomped after them, *RAWR*-ing for their lunch. Dazzlessence Jones chased after them, calling for their arrest: "STOP AND PUT YOUR CLAWS BEHIND YOUR HEAD!"

Where's Lime Green? she wondered again. She covered her eyes in distress and then peeked through her fingers. The chase carried on.

Dazzlessence leaned into Marsh, his roasted

walkie-talkie. "Calling for backup, *oooo-weee*, calling for—" Then, Mama Mazzadril came out of nowhere and ate Marsh.

"NOOOOOO!" Dazzlessence dropped to his knees and shook his fists at the sky. "I used to be a diamond in the rough. But what's the glory of a diamond in the rough if you can't SEE the diamond in the rough? I've lost all my shine, and what's worse, no one cares to listen to me at all. I've got less power than an electric diamondbrush."

"Hey," Hanazuki said, pulling herself together. "You called for backup, and here I am."

"You heard that? Marsh worked?"

"No. But as your backup, I say go show the Mazzadril who shines!"

Dazzlessence looked down at his body, which was covered in moon soot. "I need a shower."

"Don't fall apart on me, Dazz," Hanazuki urged. "Whip out that badge of yours and repeat after me: '*Dazz is back! Back again! Ooh, I feel so good!*'"

Dazzlessence whipped out his badge and chanted, *"Dazz is back! Back again! Ooh, I feel so good!"* Then one of the kiddo Mazzadrils came out of nowhere and ate the badge. Dazzlessence jetted after him. "NOOOOOO! Come back, you scoundrel! Regurgitate it or I'll put you in Mazza-jail, which is a thing I will build as soon as you let me arrest you!"

"Oh boy." Hanazuki took a deep, shaky breath and ran toward the space rave to find Lime Green. There, Pyramid Scheme was rapping up fresh lyrics to a song called "Hard Knock Moon." Little Dreamer was hovering over him, one hand to his ear and the other miming the use of a turntable. Sleepy was break-dancing on the moon floor, sporting Red Hemka on his head like a wig. "This dance-a-thon is going to give me a magic attack, H," he drawled.

"Is that good or bad?" Hanazuki asked, crossing her fingers and toes in hopes he'd say, "good."

"It's bad."

She uncrossed everything, a bundle of nerves. "Well, did you ask Pyramid Scheme to turn it down? Or to take some time off so that you can catch up on your sleep? There are lots of ways to solve this problem."

"Says the Moonflower who was too scared to solve it herself."

"I wasn't *scared.*"

He stared at her blankly.

"OK, fine! I was scared! For *you!* For *everyone!* But I left to find solutions that could make us *all* happy. I wanted to find a way to help you *and* Talking Pyramid *and* Lime—" Hanazuki broke off, sidetracked by a sudden weight on her leg. "LIME GREEN!" she exclaimed, her heart spilling over with love. "Aw, I've missed you, you squishball!"

He wrapped his ears around her. "YA YA YEE," he cried, quivering.

"It's OK! I'm here now! The dark's not *so* scary anymore, right?"

"YOO-YEE-YO!" he disagreed, shaking his ears.

"Oh. I'm sorry." Hanazuki felt another ripple of guilt cascade all the way down to her toes. "I'll never leave you behind again! I promise. You and me. We're a team. With you koala'd to my leg, we will face your fears together. And the good news: All of the Dark Siders have come over to our side of the moon to help!"

Apparently, this did not sit well with Lime Green. "YAAAAAAAA!" he shrieked, pushing Hanazuki toward her Treasure Tree serenity garden just beyond a pile of comet debris.

"You're taking us to my peaceful place! Do you want to meditate with me? That would be so special." She smiled proudly at him. "See? You're already facing your fears!

"YEE YOW YAW!" Lime Green shrieked.

"OK, Mr. Modesty," she joked, trying to take his screaming in stride. "I, for one, admire you for taking a step in the right direction. It's healthy to de-stress and enjoy fresh air, fresh fruits, fresh—" They arrived, and Hanazuki swallowed her sentence. If the other garden was a sick colony, this one was a war zone. The branches were all dried up, drooping in twisted positions to the ground. The leaves were black and laced with little white bugs. Whatever fruit hadn't fallen were as shriveled as prunes. "Wait, are all the trees growing sicker?"

Lime Green nodded, tears welling in his eyes.

"Well, then we need to feed them goop *right away*!"

Hanazuki tossed Lime Green onto her back, and, in panicked overdrive, ran to the Goop Fountain to find yellow goop, red goop, purple goop, lime green goop, green goop, teal goop, orange goop, lavender goop, ALL THE GOOP. But a Mouth Portal's slime had flooded the fountain. The goop was gone. If they couldn't nourish the Treasure Trees, they'd die. If the Treasure Trees died, then how would they protect the moon from the Big Bad?!

Just then, the Mazzadrils, followed by the

Hemka, followed by Dazzlessence Jones, ran by screaming. Doughy trailed behind them, floating on his bun in the mouth slime with a pie in his hand.

"Hey, we've got a problem!" Hanazuki said. "I need your help!"

They ignored her. Just as she was about to call out to them again, another space spam was delivered . . . smack into the side of her head. "Not now, Kiyoshi!" she burst out. She flicked the glowing blue ball aside and barely missed the Hemka, who were being followed by the Mazzadrils, who were being followed by Dazzlessence Jones, all running and screaming from the OTHER DIRECTION. Doughy trailed behind them, still floating, this time with a cake made of cupcakes.

Hanazuki climbed a pile of debris and looked down at her dire moon: the dying Treasure Trees, the menacing space spam, the moon creature chaos. The wind was whipping around her shoulders, which usually meant one thing

and one thing only—the Big Bad was coming. Trembling, she scanned the sky. It was clear, but for how much longer?

"Enough is enough," she said aloud, picking up a comet piece that sort of resembled a megaphone. She drew in a sharp, short breath and shouted for all the moon to hear, "MOON MEETING IN THE SAFETY CAVE IN FIVE. HANAZUKI OUT."

CHAPTER FIVE

MOON MEETING

ive minutes later, alone inside the Safety Cave, Hanazuki tapped her fingers on the moon-rock conference table. She scanned the empty seats. She stole looks at the door. She constructed nameplates. She began pulling out her own hair. *Come on, come on, come on, moon creatures. Sleepy? Dazz? Lime Green? The rest of the Hemka? Where on the moon are you?*

And then, strolling in through the boulder doorway was Doughy Bunington, croissant crumbs flying from his mouth.

"Hi! Hi! Welcome," Hanazuki said, trying to put a lid on the fear doing cartwheels in her chest. "Find your seat assignment, and we'll begin as

soon as the rest of our colleagues arrive. Which should be aaaany second."

Doughy plopped down in front of Sleepy Unicorn's nameplate, put his feet up on the table, and leaned back with his arms folded behind his head. "I take my coffee light and sweet: eleven sugars, half a cup of half-and-half, six pumps of hazelnut creamer, and a drop of soy."

"There's no coffee."

"NO COFFEE? I can't think without coffee." He blinked. "I'll take a jelly donut with my no coffee, please. Actually, custard. No, jelly."

"There are no donuts."

"NO DONUTS?"

"Please, just tell me now," Hanazuki said, "is anyone else coming?"

Doughy shrugged. "I'm no one's keeper."

"I asked you to buddy up with Sleepy Unicorn."

"Yes, but then you told me not to move."

"You were just floating in the moon slime."

"Yes, but then you told me to come here, and here I am."

Hanazuki rolled her neck. Massaged her temples. Tried to breathe.

"I wouldn't worry about it," Doughy said. "The rest of the gang will probably arrive fashionably late, which I recently learned does not mean showing up tardy in Armooni sunglasses. Give them an hour."

"AN HOUR?! We don't have AN HOUR!"

"I feel unsafe under this time restraint. Have you read the e-book *How to Manage a Moon Meeting*? I haven't. But I hear there's a chapter on time management."

Hanazuki slammed both hands on the table. "I'm getting started. Do you think you can be useful without a pastry in your mouth? Don't respond to that. Here's the agenda: Heal the trees, and then figure out how to cohabitate in the dark. Comfortably. Right now, we're in a real pickle."

"See, now pickles would have been a good meeting snack."

"Doughy, focus!" Hanazuki grabbed his cheeks. "Look, the truth is, I came over to the Dark Side for *your help*. My friends, especially Lime Green, were suffering. They have no idea how to live comfortably in the dark. And since you are the only creature I know who once lived on the Light Side and now lives in the dark, I wanted to pick your brain. I still do."

Doughy rose with the purpose and class of an Italian sausage. "Hanazuki, I ask that you close your eyes for just a moment while I prepare a lecture."

"A lecture?"

"A lecture," he repeated in a sophisticated accent.

Hanazuki was weirded out. Still, she shut her eyes. She heard shuffling and banging and grunting, and tried really hard to give Doughy the benefit of the doubt—that whatever he was doing was not a ploy for pastries, even though it was *probably* a ploy for pastries.

"Now open your eyes and your book."

Hanazuki opened her eyes, and in front of her, bobbing on the conference table, was a third space spam. "Are you ambushing me with bad news?" she asked Doughy with nervous anticipation. "Is this your idea of a lecture?"

"Huh? No." Doughy, now wearing tortoiseshell glasses and a sweater vest, pointed at the spam with a laser pen. "This intrusion has nothing to do with my lecture."

"Well, do you think I should open it?"

Doughy exhaled hotdog breath onto the lenses of his glasses and wiped them with his bun. "If you must. Go on. I'm not offended. I get it. You're of a different generation. Face-to-face interactions take a backseat to space spam. I can wait."

"Uh, OK. Thanks." Hanazuki was feeling even more worried. If this was the third message from Kiyoshi, then things were clearly not OK with him. *Could* she help him? Could she afford to leave her moon? What if she did leave to help and then returned only to find her moon even more chaotic and sick? *Then* what?

"*Well*," Doughy pressed, tapping his watchless wrist. "We don't have all day."

Hanazuki took a deep breath and threw the space spam against the moon-rock conference table. The ball disappeared, revealing a pixelated animation of Kiyoshi's face. "Uh, hey there,

Hanazuki." His voice was painfully slow and jittery. "I hope you're getting this. I've sent you a bunch of spam. It keeps coming back to me as 'message undelivered.' Which is worrisome. You always check your messages! This is Kiyoshi, by the way."

"Yes, I know," Hanazuki urged the animation. "Just spit it out."

"Not to freak you out—not that I'm *assuming* you'll freak out—I'm totally *not trying* to freak you out—"

"You're not freaking me out!"

"It's just that, as you know, when I look at black Treasure Tree fruit, I see stuff like the past, present, and future. And what I'm seeing presently? Well, it doesn't look so hot. 'Hot' as in 'good.' It doesn't look good."

Hanazuki closed her eyes and shook her head. *I know it's not looking good! New information, please!*

"As far as the future though, well . . ."

Hanazuki scooted to the edge of her seat and dug her fingernails into her thighs.

"It appears that—" Kiyoshi's voice was suddenly drowned out with static.

"It appears that *WHAT*?! Hello? Kiyoshi? KIYOSHI?" The static continued for thirty seconds. "KIYOSHI! COME BACK! KIYOSHI! KIYOSHI!"

"So, that's what's in store for you," Kiyoshi said somberly, his voice returning, now static-free. "Good luck, Hanazuki. I'm sure you'll handle all this a whole lot better than I would." Then his face dissolved from the table. Hanazuki looked up at Doughy in a panic. He seemed unfazed by the message, but totally fazed by Hanazuki's disruption to his lecture. "Are you done?" he asked all teacherly. "Because as far as I remember, *you're* the one who wanted to pick *my* brain."

"I'm done," she said, sinking into her chair apologetically. Meanwhile, her head was spinning. Kiyoshi didn't need her help after all.

He was only trying to warn her. But what was about to happen? And what could she do? What *should* she do?

Doughy warmed up his speaking voice with a tongue twister: "Unique New Moon. New Moon's unique. You know you need Unique New Moon." Then he cleared his throat to begin. "Living on the Dark Side of the Moon stunk at first. A lot. A real stinker." He paused for suspense. "End of lecture."

"Excuse me?" Hanazuki said, flabbergasted.

"You're excused."

"No. I mean, I get that it stunk at first. Obviously, it did! You were EXILED to the DARK. I want to know how you adjusted! How you adapted! How you made life on the Dark Side NOT STINK!"

Doughy clasped his hands together. "Well, since you are such an eager student, I will answer that in detail. In no time, I became the moon's best pastry farmer. My eyes adjusted to the dark. I

lost all my hair, and it never grew back. I slept whenever I wanted. I treated myself to crater-sandbox therapy, spending hours constructing condiment bottles out of damp sand. No one cared that I got fat. My life is a hotdog's dream now."

"*OK, OK*," she said, trying to make sense of Doughy's experience. "In what you just said, there's got to be a golden nugget for me to use against whatever Kiyoshi thinks is in store for us."

"There are hotdogs in some stores and also this story, but no chicken nuggets."

"Uh, not what I meant, but great." Hanazuki replayed Doughy's story in her mind over and over, trying to filter out the nonsense for a moral. Finally, something clicked. "I guess when life hands you colliding comets, you make, um—"

"Comet-custard eclairs."

Hanazuki cocked her head. "Sure! That's a lesson I'm willing to try. Things are going to get bad, but I can always find a way to turn them on its head and make them good." She chewed the inside of her cheek as her wheels began to turn. Sure, it might be tough to adapt to the dark, but she bet she could *teach* best practices. She bet those best practices could *inspire* the moon creatures to make the moon a better place. Just like Doughy found his passion farming pastries, she bet she could help her friends find and pursue their passions, too!

Incredibly, she saw it all play out before her eyes. "I'll instruct the Hemka to clap moon rocks to keep all the Mouth Portals awake. They'll suck up all the mouth slime. New goop will pool in the fountain. The trees will be nourished. Pyramid Scheme's rapping will be on a schedule. It will inspire new art. Sleepy will sleep. I'll make Lime Green night-vision goggles. You'll harvest Chicken Plant the best meals of her life. Basal Ganglia will occupy the Safety Cave and be out of everyone's way. Toddler Mazz will taste-test your line of meat pastries for fangless mouths. My life will *also* be a hotdog's dream!"

"Not sure that wording works for you."

"I'll find something better."

"Anyway, great moon meeting," Doughy said, shaking Hanazuki's hand.

"Thanks for the inspiration, Professor!" Hanazuki looked around at the transformed Safety Cave and thought back to the moment before the comet collision, when Dazzlessence had wanted them to hide out. She hadn't wanted to hide out then, and she didn't want to hide out now. "This moon is our home, and it's going to stay that way," she said, feeling suddenly unbreakable. "Light or dark! Whatever danger Kiyoshi thinks we're in, let's get out there and make moon history!"

Hanazuki reached the door when she heard a double clank.

"Knock knock," Dazzlessence said, peering inside.

"Who's there?" Hanazuki and Doughy joked heartily.

"The Big Bad."

CHAPTER SIX

DAZZLE BRIGHT LIKE A DIAMOND

OOOOOOOOOOO! Hanazuki and Doughy Bunington sprinted outside to where Dazzlessence was looking up at the twinkling sky. It was being swallowed up by blackness. This wasn't the first time their moon had been under attack—three moon cycles ago, the Big Bad had started to creep too close for comfort, though thanks to Little Dreamer and his bountiful treasures, everything had worked out just fine. But now?

"Yum," Doughy said. "This Big Bad fella looks like an oozing burnt pancake."

"Well, it's not," Hanazuki croaked. "It's a

dark force that saps moons of their color and sometimes makes them go KABLOOWIE."

Dazzlessence shuddered. "I hate that word."

"Me too," Hanazuki said. "It makes me feel broken."

"So, how do we stop this Biggie Bad pancake?" Doughy asked.

"*Trees, trees, lots of healthy trees*," Dazzlessence sang.

Doughy scratched his armpit, clearly unfazed by the hugeness of the problem. "Shall we go ahead with that goop plan of yours, Hanazuki? Get the Hemka to moonclap awake the Mouth Portals, and then get the Mouth Portals to suck up the mouth slime, and then wait around for new goop to feed the trees? I'd love a taste of goop."

"Um." Hanazuki would have loved to go with her original plan, but there was absolutely no time. The Big Bad was bleeding toward them faster, faster, faster than she'd ever seen.

"Oh! Here's an idea," Doughy went on. "I can

grow actual pancakes while we wait. Make some burnt ones to fit the theme."

Hanazuki shook her head. "We need Little Dreamer. We need loads of treasure. We need—"

"To go back to the Safety Cave!" Dazzlessence Jones declared.

"No!" Hanazuki laid a hand on his diamond shoulder. "NEW TREES. That's what we need. We can't hide out while the Big Bad destroys our home. Pick up your cowboy boots, brush off that moon soot, and blow your whistle. We can't waste another second!"

Insecurity flashed across Dazzlessence's eyes, but still he obeyed. "*What time is it? SHOWTIME!* Follow the freestyle, y'all!"

"That's a diamond," she said, smiling proudly.

Hanazuki, Dazzlessence, and Doughy ran through the mouth slime as fast as they could until they reached the space rave, where Pyramid Scheme was rapping louder than ever. Little Dreamer had his eyes shut and his headphones on, and he was flying to the beat of Pyramid Scheme's newest verse.

Yo, yo, say it ain't so,
The Dark Siders are here, our classic foes.
This is our turf, this is our side,
Embrace the light, go hitch a ride!

Then, he continued to rap. Louder, faster, with triple the energy.

Hanazuki cried over him, "Little Dreamer! We need you! Desperately! Please, please, please with a treasure fruit on top, drop me treasure. Like, a lot of them."

"Hee-hawr," Little Dreamer whispered, doing a flip.

"Come down with your treasure dropped," Dazzlessence chimed in, flashing handcuffs. "No one's going to get hurt if you simply drop your treasure."

"Hawr-hee," Little Dreamer whispered, doing another flip.

Hanazuki looked at Dazzlessence. "We've got to get Pyramid Scheme to stop rapping. I'll bet that as soon as he stops, Little Dreamer will deliver us treasure."

"True dat." Together, Dazzlessence and Hanazuki tried to get Pyramid Scheme's attention. They waved, they jumped, they called, but he was jamming out with his eyes shut and his headphones on.

"You can't stop the beat," Sleepy Unicorn warned Hanazuki, standing against a purple mushroom and shaking his bum in quick, spastic bursts. "If only you would have tried to stop Pyramid Scheme when I'd asked you to, when he was an emerging artist and more receptive to feedback."

"Sorry!" Hanazuki shouted. "But I had bigger fish to fry before!"

"I don't see fried fish." Suddenly Sleepy Unicorn stopped shaking his bum and slogged around like a zombie. "It's the Uni-mash. It's a terribly frightening dance. I don't know why I'm doing it. I need sleeeeeep!" The Hemka darted around his purple hooves, trying to avoid getting trampled.

"That's it, I'm going up." Hanazuki began to scale Pyramid Scheme. "STOP THE MUSIC, SCHEME!" She climbed higher, digging her fingers into the moon brick. "PLEASE! WE NEED YOUR HELP!" She was so close that she could feel the spray of Pyramid Scheme's spit as he rapped.

"I GET IT," Hanazuki called to him. "Your late-night rapper persona is SO HIP, SO MOVING, SO INSPIRING, but please, we need you to be WISE-TALKING PYRAMID RIGHT NOW. Little Dreamer will only come down IF YOU STOP!" She clawed all the way up to the mic, but right as she went to speak into it, she lost her footing and crashed to the ground.

Pyramid Scheme kept rapping. Little Dreamer kept grooving.

"Should I call for Kiazuki?" Hanazuki asked Dazzlessence. "She's on her spacesurfer, exploring the galaxy for Moonflower-less moons. Surely she can come back and help. Maybe she has old treasure from Little Dreamer lying around that she'd be happy to donate?"

"Kiazuki is well-versed in growing *black* Treasure Trees," Dazzlessence argued. "Black Treasure Trees don't protect us from the Big Bad. Also, do you really think she would let any treasure go unused? *I don't think soooooo.*"

"Well, I—I don't have a Plan B," Hanazuki confessed.

"Hmm, what got Pyramid Scheme rapping in the first place?" he asked.

"The dark."

"So then, we need to *MAKE IT LIIIIIIIIIGHT!*"

Hanazuki shrugged, unimpressed. "I mean, yeah, but I already tried bringing light back to our side of the moon, and it didn't work, so—"

Dazzlessence put his finger over Hanazuki's

mouth, cutting her off. "You once told me to show them who shines. Let me shine, H! *Let meeeee shine!*"

Before Hanazuki could say another word, Dazzlessence dipped himself in mouth slime and spun around like a tornado. When he was done with his spit bath, his diamond body was sparkling clean. "Listen up, my moon citizens," he said, bursting with fresh confidence. "We've got a Big Bad problem on our hands, and I've got a Big Bad solution in my one carat head. Y'all ready to participate?"

Doughy burped. Sleepy collapsed, just missing Teal Hemka.

"First things first," Dazzlessence went on. "Hemka, I need you to shapeshift into a squeegee—you know, a tool with a flat, smooth blade to control liquid flow—so I can push aside the mouth slime in this area. Go!"

Red Hemka flattened himself into a smooth blade while Yellow Hemka morphed into a stick.

Dazzlessence used the makeshift squeegee to push aside the slime in a ten-by-ten-foot area, and then once it was clear, Lavender Hemka, Green Hemka, Teal Hemka, and Purple Hemka formed a wall to keep the slime from oozing back inside.

"*In-cred-i-ble work!*" Dazzlessence sang. "Nice and dry and probably safe from *electrocution!*" In the corner, with his cowboy boot, he heeled an *X* in the moon ground. "Now, Sleepy Unicorn, you stand here, Man of Moves."

Sleepy slogged in a circle, chasing his tail. "Danced out. Time to pass out. Can't stop, won't stop, need to stop, bedhead, corn on the unicob, disaster."

"Lure him with a pillow," Hanazuki suggested to Orange and Yellow Hemka.

"Pee-choo!" they replied. They shape-shifted into a ladder, plucked one of the few marshmallow clouds left in the sky, and carried it to Sleepy's *X*. Sleepy galloped to it, rested his head on it with his bum in the air, and began to snore.

Dazzlessence blew his whistle, and Sleepy yawned awake. "I just had the worst dream," he said. "There were two comets and they were giving each other a high five, and then the high five was really strong. So strong that the comets exploded, and our moon went all crazy. Everything was dark, and there was rap music that was much too catchy. It was terrible."

"Sounds it," Hanazuki said.

"It's funny. I'm glad to be up, but I'm also ready to go back to sleep."

Hanazuki looked at Dazzlessence with urgent eyes.

"So, *Sleeeeepy, my man*," Dazzlessence sang, throwing him into a friendly headlock. "Here's what's going to happen. You're going to use your magic to—"

"Magic?" Sleepy asked.

"Yes.

"Oh, I'm way too tired for magic."

Hanazuki's eyes bulged. *That* was the plan? Was Dazzlessence really relying on Sleepy Unicorn's dwindling magic to save their moon?! It didn't work last time when she'd asked him to blow up the almost-colliding comets in the sky, so why would it work now?

Dazzlessence got down on his knees and looked Sleepy in the eyes. "If you do this for us, my unicorn, I swear I will build you a bed *fit for royalty*."

"I would like a moon-rock bedframe."

"*Moontaaaaastic*." Dazzlessence fist-bumped Sleepy's hoof and positioned himself in the other corner. "Now, you're going to shoot magic lightning from your horn toward my diamond body. I repeat: Your lightning, my body."

"Also, molted Chicken Plant feathers for the pillow."

"Fine." Dazzlessence plowed on. "The idea is that your magic lightning will reflect off me with such *a full-spectrum sparkle* that light will be artificially produced!"

"Also, a slime-filled mattress."

"Oh, *brother from another mother*! We're doing this, Sleepy, and we're doing it now. *One, two, three . . . SHOOOOOT*!"

Sleepy Unicorn stood up straight, pointed his horn at Dazzlessence's diamond body, made his concentration face, and fired his lightning magic. It spewed three feet in the air, seven feet short of Dazzlessence's body, and struck Blue Hemka on its way down. He teased out like a cotton ball.

"Yikes," Hanazuki said.

"Great warm-up, Sleepy," Dazzlessence said, rubbing his hands together.

"That was a warm-up?" Sleepy asked, his face twitching.

"Yup. Now for the real deal." Dazzlessence moved up seven feet. "*One, two, three . . . SHOOOOOT*!"

Once again, Sleepy aimed his lightning magic

at Dazzlessence's diamond. Good news: It reached him. Bad news: It struck Dazzlessence in the thighs. He flew backward into Doughy Bunington's bun, his legs and boots blackened with char. Sleepy clapped his hooves together. "I did it! I did it! I did—ZZZZZZZZ." His legs splayed out, and he began snoring like a beast.

"Hemka—*get in there with some pinching, please*," Dazzlessence sang, unwrapping himself from Doughy's bun. Blue Hemka and Orange Hemka pinched Sleepy awake, and he fired his magic. It shot right into Dazzlessence's body. He stretched his arms out wide. Sparks flew in every color of the rainbow, spreading light for as far as they all could see.

"HOLY MOONLIGHT! IT'S WORKING!" Hanazuki cried. "DAZZLE, YOU'RE DAZZLING! SLEEPY, YOU'RE A BEACON OF LIGHT! LITERALLY!" The Hemka who were serving as the slime-blocking walls shifted back into their

squishy selves, then watched Pyramid Scheme and Little Dreamer with nervous anticipation. Sure, the light was working, but would the music stop? Would Little Dreamer *save them*?!

Pyramid Scheme stopped rapping. He shifted the headphones around his "neck" and squinted his eyes at the light. "Well, golly gee!" he exclaimed in his wise Talking Pyramid voice. "Will you take a look at that light!"

Little Dreamer didn't change his expression—he always had his eyes shut and wore a contented smile—but he did lower the headphones to his neck, too. Then, in the miracle of all miracles, he floated down from the sky in his baby-zebra onesie straight to Hanazuki.

"Hey, snoozy man!" Hanazuki said. "You're back and ready to attack!"

"Hee haw hee," he whispered, dropping a translucent treasure in the shape of a flashlight into her hands.

"Well, that's ironic." She paused. "So. I might be getting ahead of myself, but do you think you have more treasure to spare? One is great, but, like, ten, fifteen, a couple *hundred* treasures would be fab."

Little Dreamer started to zigzag in the air.

"You can drop 'em to me aaaaany time now."

Just then, Sleepy collapsed with exhaustion. His lightning magic retracted back into his horn. Dazzlessence's shine disappeared. The rainbow sparks fizzed out. The moon turned dark. Pyramid Scheme began rapping with a fever again. Little Dreamer drifted above him, ever-so-slightly waving his hands in the air. The wind roared. The Big Bad began to bleed toward them at twice the speed.

"So," Hanazuki said to her friends. "Any *other* ideas?"

The Hemka exploded in suggestions, YA-ing and YOO-ing over each other like mad.

"Destroy a rock," Red Hemka maybe said.

"Throw a party," Yellow Hemka maybe said.

"Eat cheese," Orange Hemka maybe said.

"Chug waterfalls," Green Hemka maybe said.

"Have a good cry," Blue Hemka maybe said.

"Pop a pimple," Teal Hemka maybe said.

"Wear a cape," Purple Hemka maybe said.

"Live out loud," Lavender Hemka maybe said.

"Kiss a frog," Pink Hemka maybe said.

None of their ideas made any sense. Unless their brilliance had gotten lost in translation.

"Lime Green?" Hanazuki asked.

But there was no answer from Lime Green. He wasn't there. Hanazuki's hair pulsed. Her mood plume and bracelet and treasure, too. "Guys, where's Lime Green?"

"MWAH HA HA!" she heard in the distance. "ATTENTION, MY FUTURE SUBJECTS THAT I WILL RULE OVER WITH AN IRON FIST—AN IRON FIST THAT I WILL DEMAND YOU SCULPT

FOR ME AND ATTACH TO MY PARIETAL LOBE! LIME GREEN IS HERE, YA-ING IN PAIN, SO COME AND GET HIM."

Basal Ganglia, you evil ball of brain jam. A fire grew in Hanazuki's belly as she got ready to run. "Stay behind me, Dazz. I'm gonna need backup."

CHAPTER SEVEN

BRAIN BRIGHT LIKE A BARRY

Hanazuki, with Dazzlessence a few paces behind her, followed Basal Ganglia's maniacal shrieks to the top of a moon-rubble mountain. There he was, alone on a flat rock. "OK, Basal. You can stop yelling now."

"Well, hello, Hana*zuki*," he said sinisterly. "We meet at last."

"We've met," she said. "Like a bunch of times."

"Potatoes, pot*ah*toes."

Hanazuki circled Basal Ganglia, squinting into the darkness. "Where's Lime Green?" She curled her clammy fingers into fists. "You said he was here!"

"Did I? That's interesting." Basal Ganglia

110

squinted his eyes like he was trying to recall a distant memory. "As far as I can recall, your little booger ball of anxiety *was* here, but now . . . he's gone."

"What do you mean *gone*?"

"That's for me to know and you to find out."

Hanazuki's heart was pounding so hard, she was sure Basal Ganglia could hear it. She took a deep breath to slow it down. It wasn't slowing down. At all.

"Aren't we a bundle of nerves?" Basal Ganglia prodded. "You and your sweet-screaming stressball are like—remind me of the saying?"

"Two peas in a pod."

"No." His frontal lobe lit up. "Two nasty worrywarts on a neglected foot of viral worrywarts."

"That's not a saying."

Basal Ganglia turned burnt orange. "I just said it, so now it's a saying. It's *my* saying. It's going to be the moon's mantra. I make the mantras around here. Me. Not you. Do you know what I do to worrywarts who question my mantras?"

"You neglect them on a foot?"

"I remove them before they spread."

Hanazuki crossed her arms, trying to appear brave. "You're not *removing* me, Basal, until you tell me where I can find Lime Green. And then I'll remove *myself*. From *you*!"

"Let me share a story."

Hanazuki groaned.

"Once upon a time there was a sniveling loser brain. He exhibited symptoms of ATTMTMABP. That obviously stands for 'Always Trying to Make the Moon a Brighter Place.'"

"Uh huh."

"But that's IBUBTITD: 'Idiotic Because Us Brains Thrive in the Dark.'"

"OK."

"To give you an idea of how great a loser this loser was, he started the KODSOTMB Initiative: 'Keep Our Dark Side of the Moon Beautiful.' He wanted us to compete in photography, poetry, visual arts. A real scumbrain."

"Sounds like it."

"Sounds like it? You should have seen him! He was a fat brain with skinny lobes on either side. He smelled like kale. And he ate salt, which gave him dandruff. He ran for Cave Boss, but all the other brainy lads said, 'No, he's a loser! We need a Role Model who is also a Real Model as in a Supermodel.' And that's when all the other kids began to chant for someone else. 'SOMEONE ELSE! SOMEONE ELSE!' Do you have any idea how that felt?"

"Look, I'm having trouble sympathizing. I'm sorry you were a good-hearted loser with judgmental peers, but—"

"*ME?* THE *LOSER*?" Basal Ganglia made vague choking noises and then spit at the ground. "I'M NOT THE LOSER IN THE STORY! I SMELL *NOTHING* LIKE KALE."

"What?! So, then who are you talking about?"

"BIGBRAINED BARRY!" Basal Ganglia exploded. "What would ever, EVER give you the idea that I, Basal Ganglia the Great, who smells like organic fish bait, could ever be a light-loving, arts-advocating LOSER?"

Hanazuki gave him a blank stare.

Basal stared back, his left eye twitching.

"Look," Hanazuki explained. "You told me this was going to be YOUR life story!"

"It is! Remember when everyone in the cave

classroom was cheering for someone else? Well, that was—"

"You?"

"Supermodel Keith."

"WHAT?!"

"But I hacked the election and won instead! After that, everyone was forced to do everything I shouted at them. I was the most ruthless dictator any class of brains had ever seen. And that's how you've got to be, Hanazuki. There's no room for finding the light in the dark. It's all about making the dark darker! Life isn't supposed to be *comfortable* for your subjects. It's supposed to be *frightening*. Inflicting fear is the only way. But you're not very good at that, are you?"

"Inflicting fear on my friends? No."

"Which is why I did it for you."

"What. Did. You. Do. To. Lime?!"

Basal bundled his neurons into a wicked smile. "I struck him with fear. A fear so HUGE, it had him shaking in his squishy skin. It's all part of my COLOSSAL scheme to take over the moon."

"A little tip: It's not a scheme if you tell me it's a scheme."

"Telling you it's a scheme is a part of the scheme."

"You did it again."

"No—that was just me, scheming. MWA HA HA HA!"

Hanazuki looked up at the sky and watched the Big Bad gushing toward them. Time was running out. And if they were all going to go *kabloowie,* she at least wanted Lime Green by her side, gripping her ankles and shrieking in fear. How was she supposed to get through to a psycho brain? Be a psycho brain back?! *That's it! Get on Basal's psycho brainwave!!* "Do you want to know my scheme?" she asked.

He stopped evil-laughing and started plain-laughing. "You don't scheme!"

"No?" she asked.

"No," he replied.

"No?" she repeated with extra confidence.

"No," he repeated with cratered confidence.

"OK. That's cool," Hanazuki said breezily. "I guess you'll just feel the wrath of my scheme when you fall victim to it."

"Me? Victim? To *your* scheme? Ha! What is it?"

"That's for me to know and you to find out."

Basal narrowed his eyes. "I'll tell you my scheme if you tell me yours."

"Fine," Hanazuki said. "Let's say it together on the count of three. One, two . . . My scheme is to find out your scheme."

"My scheme is to get you to fork over your moon rulership by making you go inside the Volcano of Fears, where you'll show all of your subjects what a weak, whiny whiner you are," Basal overlapped.

"Wait, did you say the *Volcano of Fears*?" Hanazuki asked.

"YUP! MWAH HA! MY SCHEME IS BETTER! I WIN!"

Hanazuki's heart dropped into her stomach. The Volcano of Fears was no joke. As if being inside an active volcano wasn't terrifying enough, this one forced you to face your worst, scariest fears. "Is that where Lime Green is?" she asked, a lump forming in the back of her throat. "Like, already inside?"

"Probably." Basal Ganglia erupted with maniacal glee. "Here's how it went down: While you were away, I watched Sleepy Unicorn try to get Lime Green to OHFOD."

"Which is?"

"'Overcome His Fear of Darkness.' But it was a real snooze fest of failure. So, I demanded Lime Green go into the volcano, insisting, 'It's the only way you'll grow the strength to face the darkness, little lime thing.' He screamed no. So, I screamed back at him, 'BE BRAVE FOR HANAZUKI. OR ELSE NEXT TIME, SHE'LL LEAVE YOU FOREVER. YOUR CUTENESS IS WEARING THIN. DO YOU WANT TO SPEND THE REST

OF YOUR LIFE ALONE AND SCARED OF THE DARK, OR WITH HANAZUKI AND FEARLESS OF THE DARK?' He screamed yes—he would go inside to face his long, long, pathetically long list of fears. For *you*."

Hanazuki swallowed, and the lump in her throat grew to a moon rock. She didn't know what to do, what to say, how to punish Basal Ganglia for what he'd done. She figured now was the time to call for backup. She drew in a big breath and shouted, "DAZZLESSENCE JONES, SHERIFF OF *MY* MOON, TAKE CARE OF THIS BAD BRAIN!" She pointed at Basal Ganglia, anxious for Dazzlessence to pop out and arrest him, but no one appeared. "Dazz?"

Basal Ganglia began to crack up. "You think I'm afraid of a dumb *diamond*? As your RULER-TO-BE, I don't report to you or any of your friends! Especially not a sheriff who, let me remind you, isn't even a real sheriff!" He mimicked her. "'Dazz, oh, Dazz? Where are you?' HA! I can't wait for you to go inside the volcano. You're gonna cry your little weak eyes out. And then your subjects will be begging me to take over. 'We don't want a scaredy Moonflower to lead us,' they'll say. 'We want YOU!'"

"YOU'LL NEVER BE A REAL RULER," Hanazuki shouted. "I'd sooner fork over my rulership to Keith or—"

"Don't you say it."

"BIGBRAINED BARRY!"

As Basal screamed, "I EAT BARRY FOR BREAKFAST," Hanazuki skidded down the rubble and bolted toward the volcano. Swerving around a corner, she pummeled into Dazzlessence, who toppled over a telescope and crashed to the ground.

"Dazz! There you are!" Hanazuki exclaimed. "Are you OK? Wait, what are you doing?"

"Hi, H," Dazzlessence said, picking himself up in a daze. "Where's Li'l Lime?"

"The Volcano of Fears."

"Holdup—he's *a where?*" Dazzlessence whipped his handcuffs out again. "Should I use these on Basal?"

"He doesn't have hands."

"Touché."

Hanazuki felt like she was going to throw up. The fear and pain where Dazzlessence's diamond had jabbed her were sloshing around inside.

"Sorry I didn't follow you," he muttered. "I was with you most of the way, but then . . ." He gestured up at the Big Bad. "For me, *this* bad monster took priority over *that* brainy monster, and well, it's not looking promi*siiiiing.*" He kicked his cowboy boot into the moon ground, at a loss. "I really wanted my plan with Sleepy Unicorn to work. Turns out, I'm just not shiny enough. I mean, you just ran *into* me, that's how unlit I am. I guess this is goodb—"

Hanazuki gripped Dazzlessence's diamond shoulders, cutting his pity party short. "Look—

you're more than your shine and you know it. Quit scoping out the Big Bad, and instead, try new ways to defeat it."

"After every stupid thing I've done, how can you possibly believe in me?"

"Because you're Dazzlessence Jones: Moon Sheriff, Crime-Hater aka CRATER, and the kind of jewel who sticks to his guns."

Dazzlessence pushed out his diamond chest, and his confidence instantly soared. "You know what, Hanazuki? You're right. I've got this." He punched his palm, ready for action. "C'mon, Big Bad, you want a piece of me? Come to daddy."

"Well, maybe don't tempt him *too much*," Hanazuki suggested.

"Good point. I'll tone it down." He beckoned their friends. "LET'S SAVE OUR MOON, MY CREATURES! RIGHT HERE, RIGHT NOW, GET IN ON THE FUN. JOIN ME IN DEFEATING THE BIG BAD. I HAVE NO IDEA HOW TO DO IT, BUT I WILL THINK ABOUT IT A LOT OVER

THE NEXT SEVERAL MINUTES." He paused. "Maybe we should give that Sleepy Unicorn magic another shot! Maybe if Sleepy *shoots me up in the air*, I can have a man-to-man chat with the Big Bad! Meet him where he's at." He paused again. "Uh, wait, *can* he chat? Does he even have a mouth? Just thinking out loud here."

"Cool, keep thinking."

"*Oh, I will*," he sang with a wink.

Hanazuki gave Dazzlessence one of her biggest smiles and ran off, trying not to drown in her worries. The sooner she saved Lime Green, the sooner she could focus on the bigger problem at hand. As always, it was about taking one scary step at a time.

CHAPTER EIGHT

IN THE LIME LIGHT

LIME GREEN, I'M COMING!" Hanazuki shouted as she pounded the black moon rock of the Volcano of Fears. The bottoms of her feet were blistering. The wind was thrashing her hair around her throat. The smog was sticking to her lungs. Still, she sprinted all the way to the rolling-cloud forest at the crater's rim. Standing there with his toes over the edge was Lime Green.

"I'm here! Don't do it!" Hanazuki cried out.

"Ya ya yee-yaaaaaaya," he wept.

"I know. I know you're scared. Basal Ganglia is a crazy, mean brain, and he told you to face your fears only so that I'd face *my* fears. But he

124

wasn't trying to help. He was trying to take over the moon." She put her arms out. "That's your cue to back away from the edge and hug me."

"Yee yoo cha choo chee tze."

Hanazuki lowered her arms, baffled. "Let me get this straight, you *want* to face your fears?"

He nodded.

Hanazuki felt goosebumps on the back of her neck. Fears about Lime Green facing his fears ricocheted through her mind. Fears about facing her own fears ricocheted through her mind, too. Was Basal Ganglia right? If she were to go inside the volcano and freak out, would her friends lose faith in her? Would they think she was nothing but a scaredy Moonflower? Was this whole thing a nightmare? A daymare? A REALMARE? "Someone SLAP ME, please!"

Hanazuki felt a delicious slap to her face, and cried, "Eesh!" It wasn't a hand that hit her. It wasn't a paw or an ear either. It was a key lime pie.

"You're welcome," Doughy Bunington said,

somehow beside her. He licked the pan clean. "It took a lot of self-restraint to carry that pie all the way up here and only consume three slices."

"I bet." Hanazuki looked at Lime Green and then back at Doughy. "Look, your pie is delish, and I'm not mad about it being on my face, but I'm under a lot of pressure right now and it's time sensitive."

"That's why I pied you."

"Not following."

"Don't do it," Doughy said. "I pied you so you'd come to your senses. I would never venture inside a volcano, especially *this* volcano, to help anyone overcome his fears. I would only ever venture inside for food."

"You would go inside this volcano for food?"

"I'd never let a white chocolate–apricot–ginger scone with pink icing and sprinkles go to waste."

"That's . . . specific."

Lime Green began screeching: "Yeee-yeeeee

YAAAAAAAAAA!" Hanazuki followed his eye-bulging stare to the Big Bad, looming over them like spilled tar. She'd never seen it so close, so big, so bad in her entire life. She opened her mouth, ready to shout orders, to spit out a plan, to do something, but her head was filled with fog.

"YEE CHEETZU!" Lime Green yelled, suddenly lurching forward over the edge of the crater's rim. In the nick of time, Hanazuki pulled him back by the scruff of his neck, and her head cleared. "Together," she blurted. "You and me. We're going inside together."

"Is this the sugar talking?" Doughy asked. "Sometimes sugar prompts me to make irresponsible choices."

"Nope. I dunno. Maybe. It's just—" She blinked, trying to piece together a convincing explanation. "Look, if it's true that facing our worst fears inside the volcano will help us face anything once we get out, then we have to go in. I don't have any clue how to stop the Big Bad. And last time I checked,

neither did anyone else. I need to clear my mind. I need ideas. I refuse to stand here paralyzed in fear. I've got to make a leap, freak out, and then carry on! Otherwise the Big Bad will destroy us all—we'll be nothing but fried-up moon spores!"

"That makes medium sense," Doughy Bunington said.

"Great! Do me a favor, though? You seem to be oddly fast at getting places. Grab Dazzlessence and Sleepy and all the Hemka, too. Lime Green and I—we're going to need help getting out of the volcano once we've, you know, faced our worst fears and stuff."

"You've got it," Doughy said, and then began waddling down the volcano path.

Standing at the edge beside a shaking Lime Green, Hanazuki looked into the Volcano of Fears. She pointed down at a narrow, somewhat flat rock about thirty feet below. "Let's aim for that," she told him. Lime Green jumped into her arms. "On three, we feel the fear. Together." Hanazuki took a shaky breath. "One, two, THREEEEEEEEEEEEEEEE!"

They flew through the air in what felt like slow motion. Their bottoms were wiggling. The wind was beating against their cheeks. Finally, they made contact with a rock. *Thud!* Then, before they had a moment's rest, they tumbled in opposite directions . . . over the edge.

Hanazuki and Lime Green both caught the edge of the rock with their fingers and ears. Lime Green panicked, looking at the lava boiling below them. "YA YA YA YA!" he screamed.

"OH MY MOON, OH MY MOON!" Hanazuki screamed over him. "LIME, DON'T LET GO! WHATEVER YOU DO, HANG TIGHT!"

But Lime Green didn't scream another "YA!" His eyes glazed over as a series of holographic projections appeared before him. He faced his worst fears, which were:

a) He drinks too much rainbow waterfall and drowns his insides.

b) Moon critters lay their eggs in his skin, which hatch, and then those babies grow up and lay more eggs in his skin, and so on, until he becomes a carcass for bug baby-making.

c) He gets eaten by Chicken Plant and then,

living inside her stomach, hopes one day he'll be freed via an egg drop, but that day never comes.

d) He never sees the light on the Light Side again and stumbles through the dark with comet shards in his ears, shrieking for all eternity.

e) He gets hugged to smithereens by the Big Bad.

f) All his friends get hugged to smithereens by the Big Bad.

And lastly, g) He's not brave enough to help Hanazuki when she needs him the most.

This last fear wasn't projected as an image or video. It was the words NOT BRAVE ENOUGH TO HELP HANAZUKI WHEN SHE NEEDS HIM THE MOST, with an arrow pointing at Hanazuki, who was still holding on to the edge of the rock for dear life.

Hanazuki began to cry. This was too much. She didn't *want* to fall into the pool of lava. She didn't *want* Lime Green to have to face his worst fear for *real*. But it wasn't about what she wanted. It was what she *needed*, and maybe, what he needed, too. "You can do this, Lime!" she cheered through her tears. "You are absolutely brave enough to help me when I need you the most!

Lime Green grunted, readying himself. He moved one ear at a time along the edge of the rock until he was next to Hanazuki. He jumped onto her back, scurried up to her shoulders, and leaped onto the rock. Then he tugged at Hanazuki's Mood Plume, which was tightly secured to her head. After three big tugs, Hanazuki was able to put her elbows on the rock. Another three tugs and she was able to rest her torso on it. Using every last bit of energy, she kicked her legs up behind her. She crawled to the middle of the rock as quickly as possible and cried out with exhaustion and triumph, "YOU DID IT, YOU DID IT, YOU DID IT!"

"YA YOODLE YAYA," Lime Green whimpered, throwing himself into her arms, tears streaming down his face.

Hanazuki didn't have time to wipe his face dry. Like magnets, her eyes fixed onto another holographic projection—a blurry one—that appeared right in front of her. It was her turn to face her worst fears. She expected to see the Big Bad. She expected to see dead Treasure Trees. She expected to see herself fail her friends. She expected her friends to see her as nothing but a scaredy Moonflower. But as the image sharpened, she watched something entirely different: There she was at the crater's rim of the Volcano of Fears, holding Lime Green. Together, they jumped. She hit the rock. She almost slipped into the lava. She asked Lime Green to risk his life to save her.

She had *already* faced her worst fear.

Suddenly, the volcano began to rumble. The lava began to rise. She faced Lime Green. "We've gotta get out of here. Right now! HELP! HEEEEELP! HEEEEEEEEEEEEEEELP!"

From the top of the volcano, a familiar voice sang, "HANAZUKI? LIME? ARE YOU THERE?" Hanazuki looked up. Peering over the crater's rim was Dazzlessence Jones. Next to him was Doughy Bunington, Sleepy Unicorn, and the nine other Hemka.

"NICE JOB GETTING EVERYONE TOGETHER, DOUGHY!" Hanazuki called up. "WE'RE DOWN HERE, DAZZ!"

"I HEAR YOU, BUT I CAN'T SEE YOU," Dazzlessence shouted. "THIS LAVA BE *LIT*!"

Hanazuki jumped up and waved her hands until the rock began to crack. "Well, that was a bad idea." The crack zigzagged, on the verge of breaking apart. Lime Green threw himself at Hanazuki's waist, and she felt something hard and awkward dig into her side. *Wait, that's . . .* Hanazuki pulled the flashlight treasure from her skirt's pocket. It was pulsing. "DO YOU SEE THE LIME-GREEN TREASURE?" she shouted up at her friends. "IT'S A FLASHLIGHT!"

Dazzlessence pointed to her. "*YUP!*" he sang. "*OHHH, BABY, WE'RE A'COMIN'!*"

The Hemka shapeshifted into a spacesurfer, but it was too late. The rock Hanazuki and Lime Green were standing on crumbled. Luckily, they fell to a boulder. Then, unluckily, rising lava spewed out of the Volcano of Fears, and like rocket fuel, it propelled the boulder up to the crater's rim and beyond. "AHHHHHHHHH!" they screamed as they flew through the air.

Hanazuki and Lime Green were thrown from the boulder.

"MOVE OUT OF THE WAAAAY!" Hanazuki cried. They were headed straight for their friends.

Sleepy, Doughy, and Dazzlessence dove out of the way while the Hemka stayed where they were and shapeshifted into a blob. Hanazuki and Lime Green fell right into its cushy center.

Before Hanazuki and Lime Green could so much as hug each other in relief, more lava shot up hundreds of feet out of the Volcano of Fears. The display was so vast, so powerful, that the entire moon shone with the brightness of a zillion stars. Pyramid Scheme's rapping was drowned out, and suddenly Little Dreamer was on- site, showering Hanazuki with treasures! She'd faced her greatest fear *and* her tree mood was on full display. Little Dreamer couldn't miss! The treasures pulsed lime green. She threw them onto the ground, one by one, until she'd sprouted a forest of anxious, lime-green Treasure Trees.

"Look up, Hanazuki," Doughy said. "Behind you."

Terrified, Hanazuki slowly lifted her eyes to the sky. What if it was too late? What if the Big Bad was already here? What if this was the very last moment of their lives on this moon? But it was none of those things. Her eyes met the Big Bad as it retreated, a massive inkblot shrinking into a sorry self-hug. It disappeared into the horizon, and the whipping wind slowed to a pleasant breeze.

"BEST. DAY. EVER!" Hanazuki cheered. She threw Lime Green onto her shoulders. He screamed with joy—maybe a little bit of anxiety, too—and it was music to her ears. The Hemka formed a rainbow huddle around them and giggled. Dazzlessence Jones clicked his heels and sang, *"Na, na, na, na, hey, hey, Big Bad bye!"*

Doughy Bunington fanned everyone with his bun. Sleepy Unicorn was fast asleep.

"Let's enjoy this light while it lasts," Hanazuki said, finally plopping to the ground—a panting, smiley mess. She leaned back with her arms crossed behind her head, while Lime Green rested on her tummy. "It's like stargazing, but lightgazing!"

Dazzlessence joined them. "Oh, how I sparkle bright under the light!"

"So bright," Hanazuki agreed.

"Maybe too bright?" Doughy threw out, shielding his eyes.

"Too bright," Sleepy Unicorn mumbled in agreement, his eyes barely opening.

"I don't shine *too* bright," Dazzlessence Jones protested. "After everything I've gone through—*we've* gone through—there can never be enough bright light! Go on, Volcano, keep a'spewin'! *Go, go, go, Lava Lightning, go!*"

Right on cue, the Volcano of Fears started to rumble.

"Um, now what?" Hanazuki asked nervously. She flashed worried looks at Lime Green and her friends, who flashed worried looks back. The Hemka gathered around the crater's rim to "Yoo" and "Ya." She followed them to see what was up.

The lava that had been shooting high in the sky fell back into the volcano. It began swirling round and round, faster and faster, like a hyper whirlpool. Seconds later, it exploded back out of the volcano like fireworks, creating a gorgeous rainbow celebration in the sky. Yellow! Pink! Lavender! Green! Red! Orange! Blue! Purple! Teal! Lime Green! Lime Green! Lime Green! Then, for the finale, the moon started to spin on its axis.

"Is what's happening what I think is happening?" Hanazuki asked as she and Lime Green grabbed onto Sleepy Unicorn's horn. The rest of the Hemka grabbed onto Hanazuki's ankles.

And then, since Sleepy Unicorn was holding on to nothing, they all went flying.

"Whoaaaaaaaaaaaaaa!" Hanazuki, Lime Green, and the rest of her friends hurtled through the air, desperate to catch hold of something, anything, to keep themselves secure. They became safely tangled in the twiggy branches of various lime-green Treasure Trees as the spinning stopped. The moon was still. Gravity was back. And Hanazuki's side of the moon was now undeniably, breathtakingly light.

CHAPTER NINE

YIN-YANG, Y'ALL

This is delicious," Hanazuki said, licking the pink icing off of a white chocolate–apricot–ginger scone with sprinkles. She was sitting on a picnic blanket on the Dark Side of the Moon, which was, incredibly, back to its normal, Dark Side self. Around her were her best friends and saviors: Sleepy Unicorn, Maroshi Dazzlessence Jones, Doughy Bunington, all ten Hemka, and Kiyoshi.

"Yes, well, these scones are my newest crop," said a beaming Doughy Bunington. "Invented in a moment of fear."

"That's right!" Hanazuki said. "You claimed

you'd only ever venture inside the Volcano of Fears for this exact yummalicious dessert."

Doughy Bunington tapped his nose. "Fear can be a blocker of dreams, but for me, it *inspired* the most delectable treat in the mooniverse." He turned to Sleepy Unicorn. "Don't you agree? You haven't complimented me yet, and it's making me self-conscious."

"I didn't compliment you because I was too busy eating." Sleepy devoured his seventh scone, then raised the roof with his hooves. "I am so glad Pyramid Scheme is on sabbatical. My circadian rhythm is obviously still a circus."

"Oh, it'll get better," Hanazuki promised.

"I know." Sleepy yawned. "I vaguely remember being promised one moon cycle of uninterrupted REM-cycle sleep, though. And a bed fit for royalty."

"Yeah, no. Must have been a dream of yours."

"Speaking of dreams—Zzzzzzzzzzzzz." He fell instantly asleep. The scones jumped from their plate and crumbled upon landing.

Hanazuki waved a hand over Sleepy's face. She snapped her fingers near his ears. She clapped at him with moon rocks. Nothing but snores. "And . . . he's out," she said. "Where are we with the moon-rock bedframe and the feather pillow and the goop mattress?"

"Yee choo yee-ya!" Lime Green reported.

"Awesome. I can't wait to surprise him. The poor guy deserves it, and more."

Dazzlessence whipped out a shiny new badge that read: MOON SHERIFF OF THE YEAR— COMET-DEBRIS CLEANER, HANDCUFF CARRIER, AND MAZZADRIL CHASER. "And what about me?" he asked. "Look at all my accolades. Don't I deserve something?"

"You already made a new badge to honor yourself, so . . ."

Dazzlessence flashed a dazzling smile. "That I did. And that's because throughout this whole mess, I was *never afraid!* I don't feel 'fear.'"

"Ga gree chee ga ya ya," the Hemka groaned, throwing scone crumbs at Dazzlessence's face.

"Hey, OK, OK!" He held his hands up. "I admit, at unshiny times, I was a little afraid. But *darkness and moon soot can't stop me, ooooh baby!*"

"Hear, hear!" Hanazuki affirmed, standing and raising a glass of rainbow waterfall. She paused, taking in the fully recovered Treasure Trees—vibrant, perky, and healthy as ever. There was nothing more inspiring. "I think the lesson is that when you're faced with fear, go out and face it right back."

Doughy raised a scone crumb. "Yes, always leap inside the scariest volcano you can find."

"Well, hey, it worked!" Hanazuki said. "Right, Lime Green?"

He agreed with a bashful smile.

"You know, for as long as I've been living," Dazzlessence reflected, "no moon inhabitant has willingly gone inside the Volcano of Fears. Off the record, I've seen clumsy falls and intentional pushes and all that jazz. But what you and Lime Green did—*choosing* to *face your fears*, the volcano was probably like, '*What is happening?! I don't know how to process this bravery! Yow!*'"

Kiyoshi nodded. "Well, I'm glad my prophecy reached you in time! Otherwise you might never have taken the leap."

"Um . . . wait, what?" Hanazuki asked.

"My space spam," Kiyoshi reminded her. "I said, 'As far as the future though, well, it appears that the Big Bad is going to come, and you'll get Little Dreamer to finally drop you a treasure, but it won't be enough, and then Basal's going to mess with Lime Green, and then Lime Green's going to want to jump into the Volcano of Fears, and you're going to end up jumping in with him, but don't worry because in the end, everything will work out A-OK.'"

"*That's* what you said?!"

"Yeah. Did you *not* hear that?"

"Nope. But thanks for trying, Kiyoshi! So glad it worked out anyway!"

Everyone broke out into giggles.

Suddenly, they stopped. The family of Mazzadrils appeared, clomping through the thickets in their direction. Hanazuki's stomach flipped, in a bad way. "After everything we've gone through, please don't eat us," she pleaded.

Again, miraculously, they obeyed. Led by Papa Mazzadril, they clomped to the blanket, devoured the scone crumble (and the plate) and went on their dangerous, merry way. Hanazuki stared after them in relief, spotting Toddler Mazz on his grandpapa's shoulders, a meat pastry dangling from his mouth.

"Aw, look how happy he is!" Hanazuki said.

"I grew that one just for him," Doughy told the group, then pointed at a straggling kiddo Mazzadril, dragging Basal Ganglia on the same moon rock Hanazuki had used earlier as a sleigh. "And see the mean brain with eyeballs?"

Hanazuki did see Basal and noticed that he looked ridiculous. Even more ridiculous than usual. "Did you give him your crown, Doughy?" she asked him.

"Yessiree!" Doughy proudly ran a hand over his crownless scalp. "I figured if he *believed* he was a ruler, he'd stop causing so much trouble trying to *become* a ruler. Listen to him!"

Hanazuki froze to listen to Basal dictating to a nearby Mouth Portal. "Keep straw-sucking up the slime from the Light Side of the Moon!" he commanded. "Stop mouthing off! We need luxury pools on the Dark Side stat!"

"Huh, well, that works," she said. "I bet our ground will be totally dry in no time."

All of a sudden, the magnificent lime-green Treasure Tree hanging over the picnic blanket shook a few treasure fruits free. Hanazuki caught them before they landed on Sleepy Unicorn's horn like fruit kebob. "Anyone know why this tree is vibrating?" she nervously asked her friends.

"Because the last time our trees shook, there were comets in the sky about to collide." Everyone looked at the tree and then the cometless sky, baffled. A moment later, Hanazuki could make out distant rapping. "Guys . . . I think Pyramid Scheme's back to dropping mad beats."

Lime Green began to clap with glee. "Ba! Yo! Yee! Ba!"

"The Scheme doesn't seem *mad*," Dazzlessence said. "His rapping seems brighter."

"But still," Doughy said, "he's definitely doing his *thang*."

Hanazuki looked at Sleepy Unicorn, and a slideshow of the last few sleepless days of unstoppable break dancing flashed through her mind. "We've got to keep him sleeping. At least until he gets in a few REM cycles." Lime Green offered Sleepy a moon-rubble pacifier, and Purple and Orange earmuffed him with their bodies. It was everything that needed to happen. No panic, no problem.

Eventually, Doughy plucked another plateful of scones from his farm and brought them over to the group. Then, after reminiscing and chatting some more, Hanazuki looked up at the starlit sky. With the moon restored and the Big Bad gone, it felt strange having nothing major to worry about. And in a super weird way, she missed worrying. "I guess the whole flip-flop of the light and dark wasn't all that bad," she said. "Like, a lot of cool stuff happened while we were in it."

"Truth," Dazzlessence said. "And a lot of cool stuff came out of it, too. Now we've got yin-yang moon vibes *up in here*."

Hanazuki smiled at Lime Green, flopping his ears from side to side. Bellies full of sugar, her friends blissed out to the music and breathed in the fresh Treasure Tree air. It was nice. Calm. Comfortable. Balanced. Panic would always be on the horizon, ready when she was, but right now, the feels were just right.

About the Author

Stacy Davidowitz is a playwright, screenwriter, and author based in Manhattan. Stacy also teaches theater and creative writing in New York City public and private schools. Her alma maters are Tufts University, Columbia University, and Tyler Hill Camp, which she attended as a camper, counselor, and head staff. Visit her at stacydavidowitz.com.

About the Illustrator

Victoria Ying is a rare native Angeleno. She started her career in the arts by falling in love with comic books. This eventually turned into a career working in animation. She loves Japanese curry, putting things in her online shopping cart and taking them out again, and hanging out with her dopey dog. Her book credits include *Meow!*; *Not Quite Black and White*; *Lost and Found, What's That Sound?*; and *Unicorn Magic*.